Throwing Stones

A play by

Christopher John Ball and Dean Sipling

What's in your family album?

Britannia Street Theatre and Arts Publishing

Throwing Stones was first published in the United Kingdom in 2013 as an original paperback by

Britannia Street Theatre and Arts Publishing

3 / 50 Britannia Street

London

WC1X 9JH

United Kingdom

Email: britanniastreetartspublishing@gmail.com

ISBN No: 978-0-9926899-0-2

Front Cover Photograph: © 2013 Christopher John Ball

Cast in order of appearance

Stephen Giles (57)   A successful journalist and one time mentor of Adam – their relationship having soured sometime ago they now barely speak.

Nancy Lazenby (55)   Adam's former wife and now his photographic agent. She is also a gallery owner. Nancy finds herself organising both Adam's professional and personal life.

Charlotte (23)   Studying for an M.A. On a work placement with Nancy. Adam's model, muse and partner.

Adam Lazenby (53)   Published, exhibited, award winning fine arts photographer. Also undertakes society portraits which he somewhat resents. A working class boy from the north of England

D.S. Turner (26)   Metropolitan Policeman assisting D.C.I. Lydon.

D.C.I. Lydon (33)   Detective Chief Inspector of Metropolitan Police Service working as part of the Paedophile Investigation Unit.

ACT ONE
London
Present Day

Scene 1	Evening – London art gallery. Exhibition open night.
Scene 2	Photographic studio and living space. Six months later.
Scene 3	Photographic studio and living space. Next day, early morning.
Scene 4	Stage split into two. 1) Photographic studio and living space. Same day, late afternoon 2) Police interview room. Same day, late afternoon.

ACT TWO
London
Three months later.

Scene 1	Short multimedia scene.
Scene 2	Photographic studio and living space. Night.
Scene 3	Short multimedia scene.
Scene 4	Domestic Flat – Kitchen.
Scene 5	Photographic studio and living space. Early evening.
Scene 6	Domestic Flat – Kitchen. Evening.
Scene 7	Photographic studio and living space. Next day.
Scene 8	Photographic studio and living space. Two weeks later. Evening.

Throwing Stones was first work-shopped at South London Theatre in 2005 with the following cast:

Adam	Christopher Vian-Smith
Nancy	Helen Chadney
Charlotte	Laura Murphy
DCI Lydon	Emma Hillman
Stephen	Dom Lucas
DS Turner	Nick Mansley
Directed by	Anton Krause

The finished version was first performed professionally at Greenwich Playhouse, London 6th September - 2nd October 2005 with the following cast:

Adam	Christopher Vian-Smith
Nancy	Helen Chadney
Charlotte	Laura Murphy
DCI Lydon	Geraldine Garner
Stephen	Ian O'Brien
DS Turner	Shaun Stone
Directed by	Anton Krause
Set and Lighting	Stuart Draper
Producer	Christopher John Ball

This revised and updated version of *Throwing Stones* was published 2013.

Reviews of 2005 performances of Throwing Stones

"Mid-life male photographer meets young, nubile female student-cum-artistic muse - so far its old hat. But photographer turned playwright Christopher John Ball and co-writer Dean Sipling, whose background is film and television, bring the pairing into a thoroughly contemporary world of intercepted emails, sinister insinuation and sharp retorts. Their 'guilty until proved innocent' plot ... is thoroughly watchable and believable - perhaps as a result of Ball's professional insights and DS Dom Lucas' services as police advisor to the production." - *Barbara Lewis – The Stage*

"Throwing Stones has just opened at the Greenwich Playhouse and it enters the dark and perverse world of child pornography in a studied and highly creative way. Indeed, it comes close to being a totally absorbing evaluation of what some might believe is true art while others might cringe in horror at the sight of what they see is an indecent image.....Anton Krause's direction is impeccable; Helen Chadney, Christopher Vian-Smith, Shaun Stone and Geraldine Garner generate performances which are outstanding while Laura Murphy exudes sex from every pore." *Roy Atterbury – Bexley Times*

"The writers... bravely tackle this controversial subject to produce a challenging and thought-provoking modern drama." *-Bromley Times*

"This is fringe theatre at its best, experimental, vaguely existential" - *Clifford Thurlow - The New Nude Magazine.*

About the Authors

Christopher John Ball is a widely exhibited and published, fine arts photographer, writer, educator, juror and curator. With over 30 years experience as an artist - his work is held within public and private collections worldwide and he is co-founder of 'The Association of Erotic Artists'. In addition, he is also an active campaigner on issues relating to both the arts and disability.

Dean Sipling has worked in Film and TV drama for almost 20 years. His most recent credits include 'Rev', 'Room at the Top', 'Dates', 'Going Postal', 'Man and Boy' and 'Sirens.' He has served as Line Producer on productions that include 'Teachers', 'Miss Marie Lloyd' plus the award winning 'Low Winter Sun' and 'This Life +10.'

THROWING STONES

Revised 2013 version.

ACT ONE

Notes:

During the course of the play appropriate music clips (punk, new wave etc.) can be heard.

In addition – photographic images are projected at key moments.

SCENE 1

Inside a trendy London art gallery, opening night of ADAM's photographic exhibition. Photographs are projected onto the walls.

(Off stage) Loud applause and the sound of the guests milling around drinking wine, glasses clinking, piped music and babbling art speak.

NANCY and STEPHEN enter.

STEPHEN	He must have given a reason.
NANCY	Honestly, I don't know.
STEPHEN	It's not like him to miss a photo opportunity.
NANCY	Perhaps there was a three line whip.
STEPHEN	Or he received a better offer.
NANCY	Stephen, I'd love to chat about your disenchantment with the political landscape but, as you can see, I'm a bit busy right now.
STEPHEN	After the show?
NANCY	Okay. But you promise to behave this time.
STEPHEN	Scout's honour.

NANCY	You were thrown out of the scouts.
STEPHEN	Oh yeah I forgot about that…Weren't there supposed to be some pictures of Greening's daughter?
NANCY	It's quite common to make changes…

Enter CHARLOTTE.

	…Oh Charlotte, this is Stephen. Could you get him a drink? Remember, he's a journalist, so don't admit to anything.
STEPHEN	I'm also an aspiring novelist but I don't like to brag.
CHARLOTTE	This way.

CHARLOTTE and STEPHEN exit stage together as ADAM enters.

NANCY	*(Addressing ADAM)* Considering you hate public speaking you did rather well, I thought.
ADAM	*(Gesturing towards where STEPHEN left the stage)* What's he doing here?
NANCY	*(Ignoring the question)* …It's going well.
ADAM	Is it?
NANCY	*(Gesturing towards the guests)* Listen to them. They love you.

ADAM	No such thing.
NANCY	Adam, relax. It's supposed to be enjoyable. The whole night's dedicated to your favourite subject…
	(NANCY moves towards ADAM. She straightens his tie and affectionately pats him on the chest.)
	…You.
ADAM	Half of them are only here for the free wine, the rest of them wouldn't know a decent image if they fell over it.
NANCY	That's a disservice to your work.

ADAM loosens his tie.

ADAM	Perhaps if I had photographed the latest bimbo to have fallen out of a nightclub, arm in arm with an England footballer, this evening would have been a success.
NANCY	It will be. It is.
ADAM	How many have I sold?
NANCY	None. So far.
ADAM	*(Playfully and quietly)* Cunts.
NANCY	Adam.

ADAM   Sorry, even cunts have uses.

NANCY   They also carry cheque books.
                        Everyone's been very complimentary
                        and it is still early.

ADAM   Bloody Philistines. Can't you see?

                        *(He waits for a response to his
                        question. NANCY ignores him. She has
                        heard all this before. Instead she
                        moves over to another part of the room
                        to pick up some paper work.)*

                        They're just sucking up to you because
                        they're too polite and don't have the
                        balls to criticise. Except at a safe
                        distance; and then only in print.

                        (NANCY continues to ignore him.)

                        Screw this. I'm going.

ADAM turns to leave.

NANCY   *(Without turning to face ADAM)* You
                        wouldn't dare.

ADAM   Do you want to put a fiver on it?

NANCY   You know I don't gamble.

ADAM walks back towards NANCY.

ADAM   Except with my career.

NANCY	*(Turning to face ADAM)* Unfair.
ADAM	Then why invite all these chinless wonders?
NANCY	Do we have to subject ourselves to this charade on every opening night?
ADAM	*(Smiling as he has finally made NANCY react)* You love it really.
NANCY	Truthfully?
ADAM	Why let the truth get in the way of a good argument?
NANCY	It has become something of a tradition. But I am starting to find it a bit tedious.
ADAM	Tedious? You think I'm tedious?
NANCY	It's a fair analysis.
ADAM	You really know how to make a grown man cry, Nancy, how do you sleep at nights?

CHARLOTTE enters, clipboard in hand.

NANCY	Like a baby. And you?
ADAM	*(Noticing CHARLOTTE)* Depends upon who's lying next to me.

CHARLOTTE, working from a checklist, stops at set of photographs. They are displayed as a triptych.

NANCY   I don't wish to know about your sordid personal life.

ADAM   You've never forgiven me, have you?

NANCY   This will hurt, Adam, but yes, I have. It took time, but you are no longer the first thing I think of when I wake in the morning.

ADAM   I'm sorry.

NANCY   Don't be, we moved on.

ADAM   You do love seeing me wound up like this.

NANCY   There is some perverse pleasure to be had in watching you squirm like a schoolboy before an exam, yes.

ADAM   Is that why you enjoy being my agent?

NANCY   Revenge? Possibly. There's no denying you're talented. A completely fucked up human being.

               (NANCY straightens ADAM's tie again.)

               But a talented one nonetheless.

ADAM   Still carrying that candle.

                        *(NANCY pauses for a moment in her act
                        of straightening ADAM's attire, as if in
                        thought. It appears ADAM has struck a
                        nerve. ADAM takes two glasses of wine
                        from a table and hands one to NANCY.)*

                        Drink?

NANCY   No, thank you. And you should go
                        steady.

ADAM   This is only my second.

NANCY   *(NANCY takes a hanky from pocket)*

                        And how many trips to powder your
                        nose?

*NANCY hands ADAM the hanky and indicates, by touching
her own nose, he has something showing in his nostrils.*

ADAM   *(Taking the hanky)* Christ, don't deny
                        me that. *(ADAM blows his nose,
                        looking into the hanky after doing so)* I
                        need something to help me get through
                        all this bollocks. *(ADAM offers the
                        hanky back to NANCY who refuses it.
                        ADAM puts it into his pocket)* I'm in a
                        room full of strangers, bearing my soul.
                        I may as well be walking around naked
                        as they take huge chunks out of my
                        arse.

NANCY	Don't overdo it. Naked is one thing, a ranting coke head is quite another. And it's the same strangers who attended your last two previews. Show them some respect, their cheques did clear.
ADAM	*(Looking towards CHARLOTTE.)* Who's the girl?
NANCY	I wondered how long it would take for you to notice her.
ADAM	I noticed her straight away.
NANCY	Her name's Charlotte.
ADAM	Where do you know her from?
NANCY	She contacted me about her university work placement. She's reading 'Philosophical Approaches to Art and Language' and was looking to compliment the theory with something practical within the Arts. She stood out from the rest.
ADAM	I'd agree with that.
NANCY	She's a bright future ahead so please, for my sake, don't go and spoil it.
ADAM	I'm only interested in her mind.
NANCY	But it's the route that you want to take to get to it which worries me.

ADAM	I might learn something from her. It never hurts to have a fresh opinion.
NANCY	So, talk to the reviewers.
ADAM	But they don't look like her. They'll write what they want, whether I'm polite or tell them to go and fuck themselves. Let my work speak for itself.
NANCY	Leaving you free to speak to Charlotte.

ADAM walks towards CHARLOTTE. Halfway there he stops and, looking puzzled, returns to NANCY.

ADAM	What exactly does 'Philosophical Approaches to Art and Language' mean?
NANCY	I'll make a deal.
ADAM	Not another Nancy compromise, please!
NANCY	Speak to the reviewers and then, if you behave yourself, I'll take you over and introduce you to Charlotte...but only if you behave yourself.
ADAM	No, thank you, I'll take my chances without a chaperone.

ADAM goes towards CHARLOTTE. NANCY leaves.

ADAM	Wine?
	(CHARLOTTE accepts the wine without looking at ADAM.)
	What do you think?
CHARLOTTE	*(Looking straight ahead at the photographs)* I'm in two minds as to whether it's a) playful Kantian references within a cinematic framework, or b) a man approaching a post mid-life crisis who, desperate to cling onto a fading image of his youth, tries to compensate by surrounding himself with firm young things.
ADAM	Christ! Let's pray it's the former.
CHARLOTTE	I've obviously touched a nerve. *(Smiling CHARLOTTE finally turns to face ADAM)* Adam. I was under the impression you had a sense of humour.
ADAM	First night nerves. I can't stand opening nights, never could. I get edgy. Surrounded by all this lot. Everyone's a critic. Does that sound paranoid?
CHARLOTTE	L'enfer, c'est les autres.
ADAM	You've lost me there.
CHARLOTTE	It's French.

ADAM	Of course it is, but I must have been off school when we did that.
CHARLOTTE	"Hell is other people."
ADAM	Too bloody true. Present company excepted, of course. What do you really think?
CHARLOTTE	Think? About what?
ADAM	About the photographs?
CHARLOTTE	Does it matter? *(flirty, CHARLOTTE leans in towards ADAM)* Surely artists are driven. No compromises. No pandering to the desires of the audience.....
ADAM	...But are you going to buy one?
CHARLOTTE	I couldn't afford to.
ADAM	You could always...
CHARLOTTE	...Pay in kind. Nancy warned me...
ADAM	...model for me.
CHARLOTTE	Nude?
ADAM	If you wanted.
CHARLOTTE	Will we fuck?

SCENE 2

Six months later. ADAM's studio, towards the end of a photo shoot in which CHARLOTTE has been posing naked for ADAM.

The Stage is dark. A series of fine art erotic, monochrome images of CHARLOTTE are projected onto the wall.

The track 'Teenage Kicks' by The Undertones plays whilst the series of images are being projected.

The music fades and the lights go up to reveal CHARLOTTE sitting on a large sofa having just finished posing. She is buttoning up a white shirt that is far too big for her. There is a large white sheet on the sofa.

ADAM	*(Off stage in Kitchen)* Let's call it a day. Coffee?
CHARLOTTE	*(Raising her voice to answer ADAM)*
	I'll have one of those fancy teas Nancy bought me for my birthday.
ADAM	Camomile, peppermint or rosehip?
CHARLOTTE	Camomile.
ADAM	Milk and sugar in that?
CHARLOTTE	Still not funny.

Having finished buttoning up the shirt CHARLOTTE wraps herself in the sheet.

ADAM	Hot drinks give you cancer.
CHARLOTTE	Everything these days gives you cancer.

ADAM enters carrying two mugs.

ADAM   It's true. I read it in a newspaper yesterday. Though this may be the exception. *(ADAM sniffs the tea)* It smells like medicine.

(ADAM takes a sip)

Shit, tastes like it.

(ADAM hands CHARLOTTE the mug he has just tasted from. She places it on a coffee table by the sofa. ADAM sets the second mug down)

I've something to show you...

(ADAM goes over to a table, picks up four photographic prints and hands them to CHARLOTTE.)

Here.

CHARLOTTE takes the prints, lays them out on the floor by the sofa and studies the images in silence as she arranges them in various sequences. After a few moments ADAM breaks the silence.

ADAM   What do you think?

| CHARLOTTE | Good, it's really coming together. Though I think that they work better as a triptych. *(Holding up a print)* This one seems redundant. |

ADAM moves over to CHARLOTTE and sits beside her.

| ADAM | Nancy will be pleased. |

| CHARLOTTE | She has your best interests at heart. |

| ADAM | Doesn't stop her putting the pressure on. She seems happy that you're involved though. In fact, I could be forgiven for thinking that... |

(ADAM pulls at the sheet wrapped around CHARLOTTE, loosens it and cuddles up to her, playfully wrapping both of them within the material, until he is on top of her.)

...you've been planted here to seduce your way into my affections, catch me off guard and report back on any errant behaviour.

| CHARLOTTE | *(laughing)* Oh yes, to what ends? |

| ADAM | You're here in the guise of a muse, to protect her assets. |

| CHARLOTTE | Muse am I...? |

(CHARLOTTE rolls ADAM and herself off the sofa onto the floor, she is now on top, pinning him down. The work prints are still on the floor and now under the sheet.)

…I am not protecting Nancy's assets. They're mine now.

(She kisses him, playfully dominating ADAM as she slowly unbuttons his shirt.)

Have you given any more thought to visiting Paris, as a guest lecturer?

ADAM   It's not really me.

CHARLOTTE   Oh come on. You'll love it! You know you will. Give you a chance to show off. All those impressionable, young student things… hmm on second thoughts

CHARLOTTE kisses ADAM's bare chest. Slowly works her way down towards his crotch and pulls at his trouser belt buckle to loosen it.

ADAM   As my dad used to say, those who can, do; those who can't, teach.

CHARLOTTE stops trying to loosen ADAM's belt and slaps him on the chest.

CHARLOTTE   You teach…

(CHARLOTTE gets off ADAM. She picks up her mug and sits back on the sofa with her legs off the floor.)

…and you are forever complaining that in Britain it's the only income an artist can be assured of, besides the dole.

ADAM

I do not teach. I educate.

CHARLOTTE

Whatever. You do the lecture in Paris and then we can spend a few weeks together. Maybe hire a car and drive to the Loire Valley. It will be a well earned break before the book launch.

ADAM

Nice tea?

CHARLOTTE

(mimicking) Nice tea.

ADAM

Always tastes better when served in the best china. They were a gift from a ceramicist I knew. Wonderfully creative hands. She gave the best wank ever.

CHARLOTTE

Until now.

ADAM

You have, other talents…

CHARLOTTE

Careful…

ADAM

… you know how to exploit your…

CHARLOTTE	…Potential! Anyway I don't wish to hear about your past girlfriends.
ADAM	*(laughing)* Why?

ADAM gets up off the floor and sits beside CHARLOTTE.

CHARLOTTE	I don't.
ADAM	But they're a part of me, my history. They made me what I am.
CHARLOTTE	Leave it.
ADAM	I'm not comparing you to any of them, if that's what you're thinking.
CHARLOTTE	How very understanding…

> *(CHARLOTTE reaches out and pats ADAM's face in a condescending manner.)*

> …Thank you.

ADAM	My life didn't start the day I met you.
CHARLOTTE	Don't patronise me.
ADAM	I want to be honest with you. I'm opening up here, that's what people do in relationships. They talk.
CHARLOTTE	Sometimes they can talk too much.

There is an awkward silence.

ADAM   I'm sorry, it must be my bio-rhythms.
                        The deadlines. And these bloody
                        society shots Nancy insists on.
                        Apparently it raises my profile,
                        photographing Lord and Lady Muck.

CHARLOTTE   They wouldn't commission you if they
                        didn't respect either you or your work.

ADAM   Yeah right! The bastards have no
                        sooner shown me out of the
                        tradesman's entrance than they're
                        counting the family silver. Though it
                        does keep me in beer and fags.

CHARLOTTE playfully kicks ADAM in the ribs.

CHARLOTTE   You don't smoke.

                        *(CHARLOTTE moves towards ADAM
                        and places herself behind him.)*

                        Come here, I'll give your shoulders a
                        rub. Ooh feel the tension. Great…

ADAM   Ah.

CHARLOTTE   Big…

ADAM   Aah.

CHARLOTTE   Knots…

ADAM	AAH.
CHARLOTTE	Better?
ADAM	Better call a doctor. Where the fuck did you learn that?
CHARLOTTE	It's a gift.
ADAM	From the grandfather who served in the Vichy?
CHARLOTTE	No! First time I've tried it out anyway.
ADAM	Well, don't do it again.
CHARLOTTE	Nancy boy.
ADAM	Low pain threshold.
CHARLOTTE	Artists thrive on pain…

(Mocking ADAM with her hand to her forehead, CHARLOTTE playfully falls, face up, into ADAM's lap.)

…The tortured soul routine.

ADAM	Maybe the case in those romanticised biographies but in reality it's just a front for the public. What we all really want is to be happy, rich and for the sun to shine every day in summer.

CHARLOTTE	Exposé. May I quote that in my dissertation? I promise I won't reveal my sources. *(pause)* I'd noticed by the way.
ADAM	Noticed what?
CHARLOTTE	You've changed the subject. I'm not letting you off the hook. Should I arrange it?
ADAM	Arrange what?
CHARLOTTE	Paris!
ADAM	Is that such a good idea? I don't even speak French for starters. How will I give a lecture?
CHARLOTTE	It may come as a shock to you but they take learning a second language seriously.

(There is short silence as both stare into their cups. It is broken by CHARLOTTE)

	I can see through you.
ADAM	What do you mean?
CHARLOTTE	You're scared.
ADAM	Am I being challenged into accepting a dare?

CHARLOTTE	*(Flirty)* Might be.
ADAM	I accept.
CHARLOTTE	Good.
ADAM	Under one condition.
CHARLOTTE	Which is?
ADAM	You introduce me to your father.
CHARLOTTE	That's difficult.
ADAM	Are you ashamed of me?
CHARLOTTE	He's very protective. He tends to over compensate since the separation.
ADAM	And he worries I'm corrupting you?
CHARLOTTE	I'm sorry.
ADAM	All my mum ever wanted to know was "have I photographed anyone famous?"
CHARLOTTE	I'm sure she was proud of you.
ADAM	Honestly, the proudest moment for her was when my first photograph was published in the Manchester Evening Post...
CHARLOTTE	*(playfully and dismissively)* Manchester Evening Post...oh very good.

ADAM	…It was at a punk gig in '77. "Wasted Abortions" supported "The Buzzcocks". Underneath the photo was my name. She cut it out and placed it on the wall in the front room. A sweaty nineteen-year-old, covered in gob, screaming into a microphone about bringing down the government, neatly framed next to my mum's wedding photo, me on my first bike and my sister in a nativity play. Was that the spirit of punk?
CHARLOTTE	1977, I was just a twinkle in my dad's eye.
ADAM	Get out.
CHARLOTTE	I didn't know you worked for a paper.
ADAM	Work's putting it a bit strong. I got free tickets to gigs, made a few photographs and claimed my beer on expenses. Great days.
CHARLOTTE	(*Playfully pinching ADAM's cheeks.*) Before it died.
ADAM	Punk's not dead. As long as there are people like me. Sure it's got a bit older, a little bit flabbier.

CHARLOTTE interrupts ADAM, playfully pinches his sides

CHARLOTTE	A little bit flabbier? A lot flabbier actually.
ADAM	… a bit flabbier. But it's still there. The anarchy, the attitude, the rebellion…
CHARLOTTE	…the mortgage, the ex-wife, the Volvo estate.
ADAM	I do not drive a Volvo estate. Anyway so speaks the girl whose father comes from a country whose only contribution to punk was Plastic Bertrand. Punk's not dead, is that clear? *(ADAM tickles CHARLOTTE.)* Say it. Punk's not dead.
CHARLOTTE	*(Giggling uncontrollably)* Punk's not dead…
	(CHARLOTTE stops ADAM tickling her and she regains her composure.)
	…And he wasn't French.
ADAM	I thought you said your father is French.
CHARLOTTE	Plastic Bertrand, he was from Brussels, Belgium.
ADAM	Whatever. Anyway it's a hatchback not an estate.

CHARLOTTE	I'm still waiting for an answer about Paris.
ADAM	I said *oui*, did I not?

CHARLOTTE jumps up.

CHARLOTTE	Only making sure... *(In mock French accent)* ... I shall finalise the arrangements.
ADAM	How do you know that the university will want me?
CHARLOTTE	Because I've already asked them on your behalf.
ADAM	You're sure of yourself.
CHAROTTE	I am...*(CHARLOTTE moves over and kisses ADAM)*...where you're concerned. *(CHARLOTTE moves away from ADAM)* I'll take a shower before Nancy arrives.

CHARLOTTE exits. Staying on the sofa ADAM watches CHARLOTTE leave. The photographs of CHARLOTTE are still on the floor and covered by the discarded sheet.

Enter NANCY, dressed for a night out/celebration.

ADAM, lost in thought, hasn't noticed NANCY.

NANCY	*(NANCY playfully taps on ADAM's head with her hand)* Knock, knock. Anyone home?
ADAM	Oh Hi, I didn't hear you come in. I was miles away.
NANCY	Yes, I noticed.
ADAM	I had just been explaining to Charlotte how grateful I am that you put all this work my way.
NANCY	Now, why don't I believe you?
ADAM	Oh I don't know, perhaps because you're a woman and therefore always right and I, being just a man, am obviously a pathological liar.
	(NANCY smiles and nods in agreement)
	How's Cress?
NANCY	In love with Mr Brant, the biology teacher.
ADAM	I thought it was the R.E. teacher.
NANCY	No. That was last week.
ADAM	At least she's evolving.
NANCY	Have you not read any of my e-mails?

ADAM   You should have phoned me.

NANCY   I did. I sent you several texts, you
                didn't respond.

ADAM   *(Dismissively)* Texts! I meant phone
                me, talk! Contact with another human
                being.

NANCY   We've tried that. Stop pretending to be
                a bloody Luddite in the hope that it will
                mitigate your forgetfulness. Besides -
                the idea of a mobile phone is that you
                actually take it with you and not leave
                it lying next to the land-line in the
                hallway…

                *(ADAM pats his trouser pocket to
                check for his mobile phone. It isn't
                there. He shrugs.)*

                …I need your approval on these press
                releases, dust jackets and invitation list.
                Time is short, its gone way past being
                urgent, so read.

                *(NANCY hands ADAM various
                documents. NANCY then picks up the
                discarded sheet off the floor and folds it
                neatly as she talks.)*

                Now, a car will pick you up tomorrow
                at three to take you to the publishers to
                finalise the proofing arrangements with

Julie. Remember Julie? She's your editor.

ADAM   Big tits. Bad taste in jumpers.

NANCY   The knitwear I acknowledge. Hair appointment at six. Has your suit been returned from the dry cleaners?

              (Still reading the material NANCY had given him - ADAM simply shrugs his shoulders in response)

              You can wear the silk shirt I brought you from New York.

ADAM   It's not a job interview.

              (ADAM takes a pen and crosses out a name with such force that the pen goes through the paper.)

              Oh no, you are not inviting Brian Sewell.**

NANCY   Too late, the invitations have already been mailed.

ADAM   So why am I approving this?

NANCY   To keep up the pretence of professionalism in this shambles we call your career.

(NANCY- having finished putting the sheet away- looks to the floor and notices the photographs of CHARLOTTE on the floor. She picks them up)

What are these?

ADAM   *(Firmly but defensively)* I'm not entering into a debate over what will be included in my book.

NANCY   Meaning?

ADAM   I'm not compromising.

NANCY   The content has already been agreed. You can't throw things in at the last minute.

ADAM   Who agreed? I'm the artist. We're not churning out cans of baked beans here.

NANCY   Be professional. This means as much to me as it does to you.

ADAM   It's my name and reputation that is on the line, not yours.

NANCY   You think so highly of me?

ADAM   These finish the piece beautifully and we've decided...

NANCY	…This isn't how you usually work. You like to live with the images before you decide anything. These aren't finished, they're work prints. When were these made? For the last six months you've only photographed Charlotte.
ADAM	And she's the best model I've worked...
NANCY	*(Cutting ADAM off)* Well, it doesn't show in these.
ADAM	Jealous?
NANCY	Fuck you.
ADAM	It explains your dislike for Charlotte.
NANCY	I don't dislike Charlotte. She's with me, remember?
ADAM	I've slept with my models before.
NANCY	Adam, you've <u>fucked</u> your models before. It's never bothered me. Not after the divorce, anyway. This is different. *(Continuing to examine the prints)* There's not the same passion.

CHARLOTTE enters having showered and dressed.

CHARLOTTE	Got to shoot. Bye Nancy. See you tomorrow night.

ADAM	Preferably not off your head.
	(ADAM watches CHARLOTTE leave and smiles. Turning to NANCY, he finally notices that she is dressed up for a night out)
	What's the occasion?
NANCY	My birthday.
ADAM	Shit. Sorry.
NANCY	*(Her back to ADAM)* Don't be. If I was lucky a hastily scribbled card and a bunch of flowers from the twenty-four hour garage was the best I could expect.
	(ADAM gets up from the sofa and quietly goes to a bookshelf as NANCY speaks. He picks something up from the shelf and returns to NANCY. She turns around and he hands her a card and a jewellery box.)
	What's this?
ADAM	I believe the usual scenario is that you open it to find out.
NANCY	*(Nancy opens the box. Inside is a necklace)* Oh, Adam, thank you.
ADAM	No. Thank you.

(NANCY is trying to put the necklace on)

Here, let me help.

ADAM moves towards NANCY and stands behind her. He takes the necklace and places it tenderly around her neck. He pauses for second, as if lost in the moment, unsure how to proceed within this once familiar and intimate space, his hands on her shoulders. He makes a decision and awkwardly but gently pats NANCY on the back, signalling that he has finished, and then moves away from her. NANCY turns to face him.

NANCY   What do you think?

ADAM   It looks great. Really suits you.

NANCY   *(Smiling, NANCY pats the necklace in appreciation)* I will wear it tonight.

ADAM   Going anywhere special?

NANCY   It's a surprise.

ADAM   Stephen's still sniffing around then?

NANCY   I enjoy his company. It's nothing serious.

ADAM   Does he know that?

** *Brian Sewell is an infamous art critic for The Evening Standard – a widely read London newspaper. He can be substituted with a suitable replacement if necessary.*

SCENE 3

Early morning in ADAM's studio and living space. ADAM has been working all night, he cuts a fat line of cocaine on top of an A3 light box. He wipes off the remnants of the drug with his hands and licks his fingers. He places a photographic image on the light box. There are photographs framed and hung on the wall around the studio. There are additional prints – some are loose and others are mounted on card and propped up. A computer with a large LCD screen sits in a corner.

We can hear the track 'Orgasm Addict' by The Buzzcocks playing loudly from a music centre.

ADAM is about to snort the cocaine when he is interrupted by a series of loud knocks on the door.

ADAM   Shit.

ADAM goes to answer the door - leaving the bag of cocaine in view.

ADAM   Hold your fucking horses. I'm coming. *(Opening the door)* Yes?

D.S. TURNER   *(off stage)* Mr Lazenby?

ADAM   What?

D.S. TURNER   *(off stage)* Mr Lazenby?

ADAM   Yes?

D.S. TURNER   *(Off stage. Raising his voice to be heard over the music)* Mr Adam Lazenby?

ADAM	Yes – hang on a minute.

(ADAM cannot hear properly due to the music playing so loud but he is aware that it is the police. Leaving the visitors at the door he goes to turn off the music player and puts a stack of photographic prints over the cocaine in an attempt to hide it. He returns to the door.)

	What's wrong?
D.S. TURNER	*(off stage)* I'm D.S Turner. This is D.C.I. Lydon. May we come in, sir?
ADAM	Is it Cress, she isn't hurt is she?
D.C.I. LYDON	*(off stage)* It's a bit delicate. It's best we talk inside.
ADAM	What's happened? Is it Nancy, Charlotte? Has there been an accident?

ADAM stands aside. Enter D.S. TURNER and D.C.I. LYDON.

D.S. TURNER	May we sit down, sir?
ADAM	Damn it! Answer the fucking question.
D.C.I. LYDON	We are not here about an accident. Please, sit down and I'll explain why we're here.
ADAM	What time is it?

D.S. TURNER	Just after nine.
ADAM	Shit. I've been up all night. I'm behind schedule.
D.C.I. LYDON	I can see that you're busy but if I can ask you to bear with us for a few moments. We're undertaking an investigation which I hope you can help us with.
ADAM	I can help you with, well OK I suppose I can give you ten minutes...
	(ADAM sits down on the sofa.)
	...but in exchange I want my existing library fines cancelled. You don't realise how they build up until that librarian fixes you with that icy stare, then it's too late.
D.C.I. LYDON	I thank you in advance for your time, Mr Lazenby. If I can start by confirming a few details. You are a photographer by profession?
ADAM	*(Looking around him at the photographs on the wall and the photographic equipment as if he has been asked an obvious question)* You could say that.
D.C.I. LYDON	And you have a website on which you promote your photography, yes?

ADAM   What of it?

D.C.I. LYDON   Did you build it yourself?

ADAM   No.

*Taking a studio stool, and placing it diagonally across from
ADAM, D.C.I LYDON sits down. D.S. TURNER remains
standing.*

D.C.I . LYDON   Who did?

ADAM   My agent had someone design and
                        build it. I just update it with new
                        images.

D.C.I. LYDON   So I can presume you have complete
                        control over your images and how they
                        are used or distributed over the
                        internet?

ADAM   About as much control as any other
                        photographer using the medium.

D.C.I. LYDON   Do you allow your work to be
                        displayed on sites other than your own?

ADAM   On some, yes. My work often turns up
                        on blogs, forums and other sites
                        devoted to great photography. Some
                        have my permission; most don't bother
                        to ask though. It's virtually impossible
                        to keep track.

D.C.I. LYDON	How do you feel about those that use your work but don't seek permission?
ADAM	I don't mind. Okay, I like them to credit me, even put a link back to my site but in truth there's not a lot I can do, other than make sure the image resolution is low or...
D.C.I. LYDON	And you are happy for this to happen?
ADAM	It doesn't keep me awake at night, I'm all for free speech. It's a form of promotion after all. What's your interest?
D.C.I. LYDON	During the course of our investigation into a paedophile ring distributing material over the internet...
ADAM	Say again?
D.C.I. LYDON	...we have found a series of images that can be traced back to your...
ADAM	But none of my images could ever be...
D.C.I. LYDON	We believe that some of your photographs may have been altered.
ADAM	They've been altered? What, digitally? That kind of thing?
D.C.I. LYDON	Yes.

ADAM	So you are here because someone else has altered some of my images.
D.C.I. LYDON	The images in question appear to have been sexualised by computer manipulation.
ADAM	What? Has someone been giving my models bigger tits?
D.C.I. LYDON	In a manner of speaking.
ADAM	And that is a crime?
D.C.I. LYDON	Sir; you may either have not understood what I said earlier; or did not take it seriously…
ADAM	Now you are starting to sound like my ex.
D.C.I. LYDON.	…photographs you have made of children have been altered, sexualised.
ADAM	You mean to make new images.
D.C.I. LYDON.	Exactly. The term we use is pseudo photographs.
ADAM	How very post-modern …

D.S. TURNER wanders around the room, picking up various pieces of work. ADAM becomes aware of the bag of cocaine under the prints.

ADAM	*(To D.S. TURNER)* ... Excuse me, those are exhibition prints.
D.S. TURNER	These are nice.
ADAM	I appreciate the critique, but please put them down as the acid and filth from your fingers will ruin them.
	(D.S. TURNER looks at his hands and then returns the photographs to the table)
D.S. TURNER	Do you remember taking photographs of Emily Greening?
ADAM	I prefer the term "making". You make photographs, you do not take them. In answer to your question, yes, she's Tony Greening's daughter.
D.C.I. LYDON	The Junior Home Office Minister.
ADAM	I had to chase the bastard for payment.
D.S. TURNER	He didn't like the results?
ADAM	He loved them, eventually.
D.S. TURNER	Of course, how could he not.
ADAM	I bet he put the cost down as M.P.'s expenses, cheeky sod.

D.C.I. LYDON	Tell me more about the problems with this particular commission.
ADAM	Any 'problems' were down to him. It was sometimes difficult to know what he wanted. I had to do a number of sittings with Emily.
D.C.I. LYDON	Is that normal?
ADAM	Depends on the model. She didn't photograph well when he was present. Most children are more relaxed when their parents are not around. It is important to win the child's confidence.
D.S. TURNER	And Emily, did you win her confidence? *(Examining more prints)*
ADAM	Is it the Met's policy to promote idiots? *(to D.S. TURNER)* How many more times? Those are work in progress. I'd appreciate it if you didn't put your dirty paws all over them.
D.C.I. LYDON	I take it that you use digital cameras.
ADAM	For most commercial jobs, yes. I still use a lot of film though, especially for my personal projects. I feel that film still has the edge…a sense of authenticity…more organic.

D.C.I. LYDON	And the photographs you 'made' of Emily. Did you use film?
ADAM	Yes.
D.C.I LYDON	So would you say that it was a 'personal' project?
ADAM	No, not … I used both film and digital on…
D.C.I. LYDON	The negatives from these sessions, do you still have them?
ADAM	I archive every negative, every file, of every image I've ever made… *(Directed towards D.S. TURNER)* … Call it a pension plan.
D.C.I. LYDON	May we see them?
ADAM	Not at the moment. No.
D.C.I. LYDON	But they are in your possession?
ADAM	Obviously your appreciation of the photographic art is limited.
D.C.I. LYDON	I never pretended otherwise. It would really help us if we could view the negatives and related files.
ADAM	I have no problem with you seeing the digital files, I can transfer copies onto a flash drive for you, but having seen the

way your monkey handles my prints, do you think I would trust you with the negatives?

D.S. TURNER   Are they here?

ADAM   *(Ignoring TURNER and directed towards LYDON)* No. I store negatives off-site in archival facilities. What's the fascination with this particular set?

D.C.I. LYDON   If I can be candid with you, Mr Lazenby…

ADAM   *(flirty)* I am assuming no pun was intended?

D.C.I. LYDON   … In an investigation such as this we need to gather as much raw evidence as possible to establish whether or not an offence has taken place.

ADAM   And these images are part of your investigation?

D.C.I. LYDON   In part.

ADAM   I'm sure I can dig out some test prints or contact sheets.

D.S. TURNER   We'd prefer the original negatives.

D.C.I. LYDON   Only from those can we ascertain the level of software manipulation.

ADAM	What you were saying about an offence taking place; you're not accusing me of anything? Am I being investigated?
D.C.I. LYDON	Not necessarily.
ADAM	Is that a threat? If it is, this conversation will come to an abrupt end until I contact my solicitor.
D.C.I. LYDON	It wasn't intended to be, Mr Lazenby.
ADAM	*(Angrily and still under the influence of the cocaine)* It fucking sounded like a threat to me. *(ADAM stands up)* Christ, put somebody in a uniform and they immediately attempt to annex the Sudetenland.
D.C.I. LYDON	Please, Mr Lazenby.
ADAM	What do you expect?
	(Composing himself)
	It's a shock and I'm tired. I thought somebody had been hurt.
	(ADAM sits down on the sofa)
	I'm sorry.
D.C.I. LYDON	I do understand. The sessions Mr Greening didn't attend, was it just you and Emily Greening?

ADAM	Yes.
D.C.I. LYDON	Nobody else present, no assistant, her mother, no one to chaperone?
ADAM	She didn't photograph well with others present.
D.S. TURNER	Is that your normal method of working?
ADAM	Regarding this subject matter, yes.
D.C.I. LYDON	Photographing a ten-year-old girl alone. Does that not leave you vulnerable?
ADAM	Vulnerable to what?
D.C.I. LYDON	Allegations of…
ADAM	…Abuse? I may be many things, but a child molester is not one of them. *(ADAM stands, his voice raised in anger)* If you continue to go down that road, you will be asked to leave.
D.C.I. LYDON	Sir, please.
ADAM	This seems to be changing from an inquiry into unauthorised use of my photographs to something more sinister. *(There is a pause. ADAM sits down onto the sofa)* What is this really about?

D.C.I. LYDON.	Tell me more about the photographs of Emily.
ADAM	I was commissioned, through my agent, as a professional photographer…
	(Directed towards D.S. TURNER) of some renown I might add
	…by Tony Greening and his wife for a portrait of their daughter. We discussed the content and context.
D.C.I. LYDON	What about Emily, what did she think?
ADAM	She didn't appear to have a problem with it.
D.C.I. LYDON	But you have already said she felt uncomfortable.
ADAM	In front of her father. She was a little inhibited and self-conscious posing in front of him.
D.C.I. LYDON	Tell me any ten-year-old girl who wouldn't be …
ADAM	There is a special relationship between an artist and model and sometimes you have to be ruthless with anything that gets in the way of that and if I need to ask the parents to leave, I will.

D.C.I. LYDON	You never felt Emily Greening was in anyway upset?
ADAM	Not once.
D.S.TURNER.	She was totally at ease, not even bored?
ADAM	People don't tend to feel bored in my presence.
D.S.TURNER	No?
D.C.I. LYDON	No doubt you have little tricks to entertain them or bribes to keep them happy?
ADAM	That is a trade secret. Why are you asking anyway? Has she said anything?
D.C.I. LYDON	I'm not at liberty to say.
ADAM	Was it these particular images you found on the internet? The ones which have been altered?
D.C.I. LYDON	The original source material, the negatives and files, would help clear any misunderstandings.
ADAM	I'll take that as a yes, shall I?
D.C.I. LYDON	I'm afraid I cannot comment.

ADAM   I will gladly help with whatever
                      investigation you are undertaking…

                      *(ADAM notices D.S. TURNER picking
                      up more photographs and goes
                      towards him)*

                      …Excuse me. How many more
                      times…? Would you like it if I came
                      down to the station and smudged your
                      priceless fingerprint collection? Given
                      the circumstances and time of day, I
                      have been very understanding. I have a
                      lot of work to do so may I introduce
                      you to the door, your exit from this
                      building. Or do I have to call the
                      fucking police?

D.C.I. LYDON   If I can ask you to be patient; just a
                      little longer.

*ADAM picks up a white cotton glove, places it on his hand and
takes the prints off D.S. TURNER and returns them to the work
bench. In doing so ADAM is again reminded that a large wrap
of cocaine is in full view. He hides it under the photographs.*

ADAM   I am being more than patient with you
                      and your hired help. He has that look
                      about him, doesn't he?

D.C.I. LYDON   Look. What look?

ADAM.   As if he is pleading for someone to put
                      their ear to his head so that he can

	delight in letting them hear the sound of the sea.
D.S.TURNER	*(Dismissively)* Very good.
D.C.I. LYDON	*(Ignoring the insult LYDON's attention is drawn to a series of photographs)*
	For the exhibition also?
ADAM	*(ADAM returns to the sofa and sits down)* Another project.
D.C.I. LYDON	*(Pointing to one of the prints)* May I? My hands are clean.
ADAM	Yeah go on. But use the cotton gloves by the side.
D.C.I. LYDON	*(She places the white cotton gloves on her hands and then carefully picks up and examines the print)* Beautiful figure. Like me once, if I say so myself. Terrible what having kids does to the female body. How can we be expected to compete? From what you read in the papers, they get younger every day. What, sixteen, seventeen? Flaunt it while you've got it I suppose.
ADAM	She's eighteen and that particular model has a name, Justine. Anyway you look fine. You could pose for me? There is a growing market on the underground fetish scene for a strip set.

From full uniform, then down to suspenders and finally nude. Not forgetting to incorporate the handcuffs and truncheon of course.

D.C.I. LYDON   I think not.

ADAM   Shame.

D.C.I. LYDON   This print. It's the same as the one on the wall over there?

ADAM   From the same negative, yes.

D.C.I. LYDON   This one is much darker than the one on the wall. Why is that?

ADAM   Photography is like any other art. Expression, emotion, feeling, etc. I print according to the mood I'm in at the time.

D.C.I. LYDON   And is the darker print the most recent?

ADAM   Yes.

D.C.I. LYDON   Then there is no mystery as to why it is much darker.

ADAM   A joke? Is the ice maiden melting?

(ADAM waits for a response from D.C.I. LYDON. When none is forthcoming he continues)

The negative could be likened to a musical score, with the print being the performance. Naturally the performance differs according to the performer, mood, surroundings, etc.

D.C.I. LYDON   Very eloquent.

ADAM   In truth I cannot claim that as an original Adam. It's by…

D.C.I. LYDON   …Ansel Adams, I know.

ADAM   You've been keeping things from me.

D.C.I. LYDON   No. You have been making assumptions.

ADAM   There's more to you than meets the eye. What say we get rid of the sea monkey; you can correct any other assumptions I might have made?

D.C.I. LYDON   If we can stick to the matter in hand.

ADAM   Should I consider that a slap down or foreplay?

D.C.I. LYDON   *(Ignoring the comment)* So your prints are influenced according to the mood you are in?

ADAM   Yes. Like any artist I …

D.S. TURNER	Tell me. What kind of mood were you in when you printed the photographs of Emily?
ADAM	What?
D.C.I. LYDON	Well given that, as you have already stated, the image can differ from print to print, you can perhaps now understand why I must have sight of the original negatives. So we can interpret from the original score, so to speak.
ADAM	Very clever; 'Ms.' Lydon.
D.C.I. LYDON	That's D.C.I. Lydon.
ADAM	Of course it is.
D.C.I. LYDON	The negatives?
ADAM	No way. Detective ---- Chief ---- Inspector ----- Lydon.
D.C.I. LYDON	Be reasonable, sir.
ADAM	If you want them, bring a court order.

D.S. TURNER has continued to look around the studio as LYDON talked to ADAM. D.S. TURNER is now stood behind the sofa directly behind ADAM.

D.S. TURNER	Is that a path you would like to go down? You never know what we might find…

ADAM looks worried, has D.S. TURNER seen the cocaine?

D.C.I. LYDON	*(Looking at a computer)* … Looks expensive…
	(Gestures towards the computer)
	…The computer, it looks expensive. I've recently bought one for my eldest.
ADAM	I use it for my work. Your point?
D.S. TURNER	What kind of work?
	(D.S. TURNER throws two books he has taken from the bookcase onto the coffee table near D.C.I. LYDON. One by Sally Mann and another by David Hamilton.)
	Stuff like this?
ADAM	I thought I told you not to go through my personal belongings.
D.C.I. LYDON	*(Looking at the books)* You find this type of imagery acceptable?
ADAM	Of course.
D.C.I. LYDON	About that court order.

SCENE 4

The stage is split.

On one part of the stage sits ADAM in a police interview room and this is unlit.

The other is part of ADAM's studio and living space. This is fully lit and we can see CHARLOTTE hurriedly packing a suitcase that rests on the sofa. NANCY enters carrying two mugs of coffee – she hands one to CHARLOTTE.

NANCY   What time's your flight?

CHARLOTTE   Six thirty.

NANCY   Heathrow?

CHARLOTTE   Yes.

NANCY   It's ten to eleven.

CHARLOTTE   So?

NANCY   So, there's no need to rush. Take some time to think. What about college?

CHARLOTTE   I'm leaving, Nancy.

NANCY   Fine. But let's talk first. We've plenty of time before your plane. If you still feel the same, I'll drive you to the airport myself.

CHARLOTTE   He rang you, Nancy.

NANCY	Yes, he did.
CHARLOTTE	I was at the police station. He refused to see me but he rang you.
NANCY	I'm his agent.
CHARLOTTE	And I was his lover.
NANCY	Was? Seems final.
CHARLOTTE	What do you care? You'll be glad to see the back of me.
NANCY	It's not what you think.
CHARLOTTE	No, it never is. *(Pause)* You will stick by him?
NANCY	Obviously.
CHARLOTTE	No doubts?
NANCY	I've known him too long, Charlotte. He has no secrets from me.
CHARLOTTE	How comforting. I thought the same.
NANCY	It's not like that.
CHARLOTTE	There you go again.
NANCY	I'm sorry, I don't mean to upset you. Adam thinks the world of you.

CHARLOTTE

So am I one of those secrets he shares with you? He talks to you about me? A cosy little chat with his ex-wife about his new bit of fluff. Why can't you let him go?

NANCY

Like you're about to do?

CHARLOTTE

It's different.

NANCY

Yes, it is different. You're not letting go, you're running away and not from Adam.

CHARLOTTE

Standby for more "Nancy knows best, right after the break".

(CHARLOTTE cannot close the suitcase. After a few attempts she gives up, sits on the sofa and begins to cry)

He called you, Nancy....he called you....that is how much he thinks of me.

NANCY takes a tissue from a box on the table; walks over to CHARLOTTE and hands it to her.

NANCY

He loves you. And you wouldn't be hurting like this, if you didn't care. I've seen him with other women. The way he behaves, the way he speaks to them. You're special. Did you know when you leave the room his eyes

	follow you to the door and don't move until you come back in?
CHARLOTTE	The things they say he has done. It's…
NANCY	*(Interrupting CHARLOTTE)* He's done nothing. Never forget that. It's all a huge misunderstanding.
CHARLOTTE	Then why has he shut me out? Was he ashamed of seeing me at the police station? Did he feel guilty or have something to hide?
NANCY	Maybe he was just trying to protect you. Keep you out of it. If you leave now, it will destroy him. Is that what you want?
CHARLOTTE	Don't play the guilt card on me, Nancy. I can't take it at the moment.
NANCY	Don't rush into anything.

CHARLOTTE gets up from the sofa and goes to pick up some more of her belongings. NANCY remains seated.

CHARLOTTE	I just want to get away.
NANCY	And how will that look?
CHARLOTTE	To Adam or the police?
NANCY	Adam, of course.

CHARLOTTE	What really sickens me is what was on his mind when I was naked in front of him? Was he comparing me? Wishing I was different? Younger?
NANCY	That's enough.
CHARLOTTE	It's how I feel.

NANCY gets up from the sofa and snaps angrily.

NANCY	Stop being so fucking selfish. You are not the victim here, Charlotte.
CHARLOTTE	I dread to think who is. The police made me feel so guilty. The way they looked at me. And I've got nothing to do with it.
NANCY	And neither has Adam.
CHARLOTTE	They don't do this for fun. They know something we don't, or at least I don't.
NANCY	How can you stand there and say that? No matter what you think of me you must realise I would never take part in anything as sick as this. I believe Adam is innocent. And so do you.
CHARLOTTE	There you go again; telling me what I...

NANCY	...I do have a child by him. Do you think that I would allow him anywhere near her if I had any doubts?
CHARLOTTE	You don't understand.
NANCY	Try me.
CHARLOTTE	I feel dirty, used, betrayed. I feel ashamed.
NANCY	Have you stopped for one second, during your little self centred, melodramatic half hour, to think what Adam is going through right now?

CHARLOTTE storms off stage leaving NANCY on stage.

The LIGHTS go down on the side of the stage representing ADAM's studio and are raised on the side that represents the Police Interview Room. ADAM, LYDON and TURNER are sat at a table. There is a microphone on the table along with sheets of paper, books and folders.

D.S. TURNER	You confirm these books are yours. For the purposes of the tape I am showing Mr Lazenby the two books taken from his premises this morning. One entitled "At Twelve: Portraits of Young Women" by Sally Mann and "Dreams Of A Young Girl" by David Hamilton.
ADAM	Yes, they're classics of their genre.

D.S. TURNER   You purchased them yourself?

ADAM   All by myself. It may come as a surprise but I also dress myself, including shoelaces. Toilet training's also going well. Although my girlfriend hates it when I leave the seat up.

D.S. TURNER   Are you aware of the contents of these books…

ADAM   No, I often buy books I haven't looked at.

D.S. TURNER   …and that these publications include photographs of children.

ADAM   Yes.

D.C.I. LYDON   Naked children.

ADAM   Mostly, yes.

D.S. TURNER   You don't seem shocked?

ADAM   Why should I ?

D.C.I. LYDON   You don't find them obscene?

ADAM   Define obscene.

D.S. TURNER   Section 1 of the Obscene Publications Acts states that *(Reading from a sheet of paper)* an article shall be deemed to be obscene if its effect or (where the article comprises two or more distinct items) the effect of any one of its items is, if taken as a whole, such as to tend to deprave and corrupt...

ADAM

(Addressing D.S. TURNER)...what the servants? Corrupt the below stairs staff? I thought all such outdated nonsense had been dismissed with the Lady Chatterley trial. Jesus! *(Turning to address D.C.I. TURNER)* I like to think our society has progressed since the sixties. Tell me, as a public servant, do you feel corrupted? I believe that obscenity is in the eye of the beholder. Now if you're feeling dirty, may I suggest you take a shower?

D.C.I. LYDON

Mr Lazenby...

ADAM

I would be more than happy to scrub your back.

D.C.I. LYDON

I'm glad to see you're taking this seriously, I can assure you that we are.

ADAM

That's the joke. What if we took a peek at your family photo album?...

(Addressing D.C.I. LYDON)

...You have children. You must have photographs of them? In the bath? The paddling pool? Dressed as shepherds in the school nativity play. Or the classic "baby on the rug" shot. I bet your parents have similar images of you. The ones they always dug out to embarrass you when you brought the new boyfriend round for tea.

D.C.I. LYDON   They are perfectly innocent.

ADAM   Apparently that would depend upon who is setting the rules of interpretation. You admit to having such images of your children. Given that this interview is being recorded, is that wise?

D.C.I. LYDON   We are talking about differing types of images.

ADAM   Who says so? Why are your images innocent and yet mine or the ones in these books, somehow, are not?

D.C.I. LYDON   The photos of my children remain in my family album. By putting your work into the public domain, is it not fair to suggest that you have some responsibility for how they are used?

ADAM   I can't control what others read into my work.

D.S. TURNER   Has it not crossed your mind during these sessions with underage girls that they may not be seen as works of art, but as child pornography?

ADAM	Never.
D. S. TURNER	Isn't that naïve?
ADAM	Bored now.
D.C.I. LYDON	Mr Lazenby, you have in your possession photographs of children posing naked in a manner which could be construed…
ADAM	Or misconstrued…
D.C.I. LYDON	… in the eyes of the law, as being obscene. Where did you purchase the books?
ADAM	Foyles, Charing Cross Road, second floor, under the section marked "Art"…

The LIGHTS go down on the side of the stage representing the police interview room and are raised on the side that represents ADAM's studio. NANCY is still present – sat on the sofa. CHARLOTTE enters producing a letter.

CHARLOTTE	Explain this. *(Handing NANCY a letter)*

NANCY   You shouldn't have gone through my
                 things, Charlotte.

CHARLOTTE   Look at it.

NANCY   *(Taking the letter)* This is personal
                 correspondence.

CHARLOTTE   Perhaps you need to be more careful
                 where you file it.

NANCY   It's none of your business.

CHARLOTTE   It is my fucking business.

NANCY   Really? What were you looking for
                 anyway?

CHARLOTTE   Answers.

NANCY   And you thought the best place to look
                 would be in my office. You've
                 disappointed me, Charlotte. Look at the
                 date on this… it's ancient history…

CHARLOTTE   …I don't give a fuck how old it is.
                 What does it mean?

NANCY   Money; for those who know how to
                 play the system.

                 *(CHARLOTTE sits down on the sofa
                 next to NANCY and gestures to her -
                 an indication that she wants NANCY to
                 carry on explaining)*

A case came to court where a teacher was convicted of abusing his pupils. It seems that he had been abusing children for some time. Concerns had been raised by staff at the school but these had been ignored. It was later ruled, in a public enquiry, that the educational authority had been negligent in its duty of care towards the children.

CHARLOTTE   Why contact Adam?

NANCY   He was a pupil in one of the classes. Solicitors send letters, like this, to seek out potential clients for criminal compensation. Adam was invited to join a group litigation action against the educational authority. He saw it as nothing more than ambulance chasing. It is all about money and Adam wanted no part of it. It would have opened up old wounds. It should have been thrown in the bin.

CHARLOTTE   But it wasn't. *(pause)* So Adam was abused as a child?

NANCY   *(pause)* Yes

CHARLOTTE   He never said anything.

NANCY   It's not something you broadcast. He only opened up to me recently. He's obviously done his best to forget it.

CHARLOTTE	All these secrets.
NANCY	Now you know. And now know why you should stay. This whole thing complicates matters for him.
CHARLOTTE	In what way?
NANCY	I'm sure that the police will know about this. *(NANCY points to the letter)* They will have access to the original case records and the public enquiry documents. And information is shared between the police, solicitors, social services and educational authorities.
CHARLOTTE	But how does this complicate matters for Adam. He was the victim after all?
NANCY	Look, last year he was commissioned to undertake a portrait of a high profile client. A Government Minister's daughter.
CHARLOTTE	What's so remarkable about that?
NANCY	He was very precise in his idea of how the image should be.
CHARLOTTE:	Naked?
NANCY:	Yes.
CHARLOTTE	Did Adam do any sessions?

NANCY   Yes. Well, it's not like he hadn't done
               similar sessions before.

CHARLOTTE   And?

NANCY   On the opening day the father, Tony
               Greening, came to see me and insisted
               that the images of his daughter be
               removed from the exhibition.

CHARLOTTE   So, he didn't want his daughters
               pictures to be shown.

NANCY   He had originally given his permission
               for two portraits to be used. But it's not
               just that he withdrew permission. It
               was the way he acted. He came
               personally to see me at the gallery
               because he also wanted the negatives
               from each shoot.

CHARLOTTE   Why ask for the negatives?

NANCY   Greening must have known about these
               investigations months before the police
               contacted Adam. In a few months time
               there's a General Election and his seat
               is in a marginal constituency. He may
               have been trying to reduce the risk of
               any potentially adverse publicity.
               Anyway, Adam refused to give away
               the negatives of the photo sessions. It
               isn't normal for a photographer to hand
               over negatives and we both know what

Adam can be like. Proud. Pigheaded. Though I am sure he would claim...

CHARLOTTE/NANCY *(smiling together)*... artistic integrity.

NANCY   And he believes that if he gives them up, it's not a great leap of imagination for them to go missing; saving Greening from any potential embarrassment.

CHARLOTTE   This isn't Hollywood, Nancy. Conspiracy theories play better in films...

NANCY   Maybe so – but that is how Adam's mind works. In some ways it is understandable. After all, he was let down by those who should have supported and protected him. His childhood experiences have left him very distrustful of anyone in authority. For all Adam's bravado there is still a little boy inside who is hurting and sometimes, that little boy kicks out.

CHARLOTTE   I still don't understand the connection between Adam being abused in the past and the police action today. You say that it complicates things for him. How?

NANCY   There is a commonly held belief that some victims of sexual abuse can go on

to abuse when adults and the police
may…

CHARLOTTE   Fuck! So Adam may have abused
                  Greening's daughter?

NANCY   Let's both pretend that you never said
                  that.

*The LIGHTS go down on the side of the stage representing
ADAM's studio and are raised on the side that represents the
Police Interview Room. ADAM, LYDON and TURNER are
still sat at a table as the interview continues.*

ADAM   Is it so difficult for you to believe? Yes,
                  she was my wife. Yes, she is the mother
                  of my daughter. Yes, she is my agent
                  and yes, although divorced, we still
                  remain very good friends.

D.S. TURNER   And your daughter?

ADAM   Cress.

D.S. TURNER   Your daughter Cress, she is twelve
                  years old.

ADAM   And eleven months, two weeks and
                  five days.

D.S TURNER   And you would be happy for your
                  daughter to pose in this manner?

ADAM   Of course, she already has…

(ADAM realises how his words could be taken.)

…The images made by Sally Mann; if you look at them through the eyes of a parent, instead of a fully paid-up member of the Central London Branch of the Spanish Inquisition, you will see them as nothing more than graceful studies of childhood, by a loving parent who happens to be an artist.

D.S. TURNER   So, in addition to your private commissions, you have photographed your daughter in a style similar to the photographs in the two books?

ADAM   Christ, has this become an investigation into plagiarism now? I have my own style, thank you very much…

(Composing himself)

...Like any other artist I draw upon my life as source material and as Cress is a major part of if, of course I photograph her. Is that a crime now?

D.S TURNER   And do you show these to anybody else?

ADAM   Yes. I'm proud of the images, proud of my work and I'm proud of my daughter.

D.S. TURNER   Who do you show these images to?

ADAM	The usual suspects, relatives, ex-wife, agent and friend and the thousands who attended an exhibition in New York.
D.S TURNER	And your work... sells?
ADAM	I am a professional photographer with an international reputation and my work is much sought after by collectors. I also have to eat, pay bills and find ways to fund my lifestyle. So yes; I do sell work.
D.C.I.LYDON	You've talked about your personal projects and how you prefer to use film.
ADAM	For the most part, yes I prefer to use film. It has an...
D.S.TURNER	...authenticity, yes you said.
ADAM	So you were paying attention.
D.S.TURNER	I was indeed. Tell us about your working methods when using film. It is of interest because you seem to set these images apart from your other work.
ADAM	I cut my teeth on film, still have a great affection for it, the working process and its look.
D.S.TURNER	Do you scan each negative into a computer and print them digitally...

ADAM

Not with film, no. Some of my negatives are never scanned. To keep that authentic feel I prefer traditional printing, in a darkroom. Especially if they are to be exhibited or if they are intended for the more serious collectors.

D.C.I.LYDON

Do you have a list of these 'more serious collectors'?

ADAM

I don't want my clients being contacted by your mob.

D.S TURNER

Are you trying to protecting them, or yourself?

ADAM

I'm trying to defend my reputation.

D.C.I.LYDON

And what of your models' reputation? They are only children after all. Surely you have a duty of care towards them?

ADAM

Their parents signed the model release.

D.S. TURNER

(producing a photograph of a naked child running towards a tree) Did the parents sign a model release for this child?

ADAM

(Looking at the photograph) It's in a public park. I didn't need one.

D.S.TURNER

Not even as a courtesy towards the parents and child?

(D.S. TURNER waits for a response from ADAM. None is forthcoming)

This image has been purchased from you, digitally altered and passed around for the enjoyment of paedophiles. *(D.S. TURNER, his voice raised, points towards ADAM)* And you have denied the parents a right to have a say in it.

There is a short awkward silence that is broken by D.C.I. LYDON.

D.C.I. LYDON	Tell me about Peter Collins.
ADAM	Who is...?
D.C.I. LYDON	Are you saying that you don't know him?
ADAM	Who the hell is he?
D.C.I. LYDON	According to our investigations, he is one of your clients.
ADAM	Maybe, you would have to ask Nancy.
D.C.I. LYDON	I'm asking you.
ADAM	Not offhand, no.
D.C.I. LYDON	So you could not say, for certain, if you had sold him any photographs or not?

ADAM	Leave my clients out of this. If he is one of my clients.
D.C.I. LYDON	What if I told you that you had sold photographs of Cressida to Mr Collins and that he is a known paedophile. When it comes to images of children we think of Collins as being one of the...what was the phrase you used...'more serious collectors'
ADAM	What?
D.C.I. LYDON	Should somebody like Peter Collins be kept out of this enquiry?
ADAM	I've never sold photographs to such a person.
D.C.I. LYDON	How can you be so sure now? A moment ago you claimed that you didn't know.
ADAM	How do you know I have sold photographs to this man?
D.C.I. LYDON	During the course of investigating Mr Peter Collins, along with others whom we know you have also sold photographs of children to...
ADAM	...How can you know that.. ?
D.C.I. LYDON	... If you would let me finish, Mr. Lazenby. We have means of tracking

and monitoring their activities. The sites they visit, credit cards used, etc. Your work has proved to be very popular with them, by the way.

ADAM

What?

D.C.I. LYDON

We have also been tracking their e-mail. Including that addressed to you.

ADAM

I'm not in the habit of corresponding with perverts.

D.S TURNER

Actually, you are.

D.C.I. LYDON

We have copies of e-mails and orders for photographs sent by, amongst others, Peter Collins to you. We also have return e-mail from you acknowledging the order.

ADAM

But I deal with hundreds of clients. How am I expected to know their sexual orientation?

D.C.I. LYDON

The photographs of your daughter. You can confirm your wife is aware of them?

ADAM

She is my agent and Cress's mother, what do you think?

D.S. TURNER

Is that yes, she has seen them or no, she hasn't?

ADAM

She's seen them.

D.S. TURNER	All of them?
ADAM	Yes.
D.S TURNER	Every print off every negative, every file?
ADAM	Look; I've already said that it is very rare for any photographer to print, let alone show every image made from a photo session. Part of the artistic process is selection. Am I being accused of bad taste now?
D.S TURNER	And how do you make that selection?
ADAM	You expect me to explain the artistic process - again?
D.C.I. LYDON	If you would be kind enough to indulge us - again.
ADAM	It's part instinct, part aesthetic judgement, part metaphysical, part...
D.S. TURNER	*(Cutting ADAM off mid sentence)* How did you select the images which were finally sold to Tony Greening?
ADAM	By using all of the above.
D.C.I. LYDON	How did you select this one? *(she takes a photo from a folder)* Was it the composition of the little girl on her

	knees in front of the man holding his erect penis?
ADAM	What?
D.C.I. LYDON	Or this one? Where the child is lying naked as two boys urinate on her.
ADAM	I don't understand.
D.C.I. LYDON	We have another aesthetically pleasing photo here. Did you force her to wear the mask or was she so fucking comfortable and relaxed in your godlike presence to do anything you asked of her? Look at it. Tell me, Mr Lazenby. I'm intrigued to hear what metaphysical selection process you used to print and publish these images on the internet?
ADAM	*(Puzzled)* These are not my photographs.
D.C.I. LYDON	*(Angrily)* Until we have sight of your negatives, all the evidence suggests that they are. *(Pausing to compose herself)* Adam. Everyone has tried very hard to give you the benefit of the doubt here, but I for one am looking for some co-operation. I want the negatives.
ADAM	*(Long pause)* I need to phone my solicitor.

(Lights fade)

END OF ACT ONE

THROWING STONES

Revised 2013 version.

ACT TWO

Notes:

During the course of the play appropriate music clips (punk, new wave etc.) can be heard.

In addition – photographic images are projected at key moments.

SCENE 1

Multimedia scene played out through a combination of pre prepared "Weegee*" style photographs of ADAM being attacked by a two men outside a public house at night. These images are projected rapidly, in sequence, onto stage walls.

Sounds of ADAM being attacked, and struggling, can also be heard. 'Anarchy in the UK' is played over the images.

(First we hear the original version by The Sex Pistols – this then segues into a cover version, played on piano, gently sung by a female vocalist) is played over the images.

*Weegee was the pseudonym of Arthur Fellig (June 12, 1899 - December 26, 1968), an American photographer and photojournalist, known for his stark black and white street photography and photographs of crime scenes, car-wreck victims in pools of their own blood, overcrowded urban beaches and various other grotesque studies of the darker side of life hidden within the everyday.

SCENE 2

ADAM enters his studio. It is late at night. The sound of rain falling on the window pane. He stumbles into the kitchen, takes a packet of frozen peas from the freezer and places them on his eye. He collapses on the sofa. After a slight pause NANCY enters dressed in her night wear. NANCY hasn't noticed ADAM, she pours herself a glass of water and walks back towards the bedroom.

ADAM   Don't you just love this time of night?

NANCY   Adam? *(jumps slightly)* I didn't hear you come in. *(She turns on the table lamp)* You don't mind, do you? The thought of driving back to the house tonight didn't appeal and Cressida was tired.

ADAM   It's fine.

                        (ADAM sits up. NANCY sees his injuries and automatically fetches a first aid box. She sits next to ADAM. It appears to be a well rehearsed routine and indicates that this isn't the first time NANCY has had to tend to ADAM's wounds after a fight.)

                        Don't say it.

NANCY   What?

ADAM   This is going to sting a little.

NANCY   This is going to sting a little. *(ADAM winces as NANCY starts to clean his wounds)* Shall I kiss it better?

           (ADAM refuses to play the game and pulls away)

           They must have really hurt you this time.

ADAM   Leave it!

NANCY   The worst of all injuries, a damaged ego.

She tenderly nurses his wounds in silence. At one point as she dabs his wounds, ADAM reacts and pulls away.

ADAM   Jesus, that hurts.

NANCY   Shhh! You'll wake Cressida. And you - don't be a baby. It's a natural disinfectant and much better than the other stuff.

ADAM   Natural doesn't automatically mean an improvement. *(Pause)* Has she left?

NANCY   Yes.

ADAM   Any message?

NANCY   None which you need to hear right now. I drove her to the airport.

ADAM   At great speed, no doubt.

NANCY   That's not fair, Adam.

ADAM   And then there were none.

NANCY   Who did this to you?

ADAM   I tripped. She's taken her things?

NANCY   Yes.

ADAM   That's that then.

NANCY   It would appear so. *(Examining the wounds)* I'm calling the police.

ADAM   Why? Will they bring her back?

NANCY   Be serious, Adam.

NANCY, having finished tending ADAM's wounds, puts the first aid box away by the side of the sofa.

ADAM   I am. Yes, call the police. It's a great idea, I'm sure D.C.I. Lydon and her cronies will run straight over with tea and sympathy.

NANCY   Adam, you were assaulted.

ADAM   By a couple of drunks in a pub. It's not the first time.

NANCY	Why is it when you mix men and alcohol they lose all ability to communicate and have to resort to their fists? What was is this time? Football, politics or what colour is the new black?
ADAM	If you must know, they called me a nonce.
NANCY	A what?
ADAM	A nonce. It's what the working classes call a paedophile. It's easier to spell. They make terrible Scrabble players.
NANCY	That's outrageous.
ADAM	I know. As a lecturer .... *(checking himself)* .... former lecturer I'll be blamed for the illiteracy of the masses too.
NANCY	How can they do this? Be the judge, jury and executioner. What gives them the right?
ADAM	Call it male intuition.
NANCY	I call it mob rule. Have they nothing better to do?
ADAM	It's not their fault. They still hold to the naïve view that the tabloids print the

truth; and that there's no smoke
without fire.

NANCY   That's just an excuse for these sorts of
people to attack innocents.

ADAM   What sort of people? I come from the
same background, in case you've
forgotten.

NANCY   You can't condone their behaviour.

ADAM   I can understand it.

NANCY   You do have rights, Adam.

ADAM   England, my country, the land of the
free. Innocent until proven guilty.
Now who's being naïve? I cannot
believe she left.

NANCY   At least you know who your friends
are.

ADAM   Who can blame her? Paris is beautiful
in spring.

NANCY   I remember. Top tip, never agree to
meet your lover beneath the Eiffel
Tower.

ADAM   It sounded so romantic.

NANCY	It was. Though your constant comparisons to Blackpool Tower did rather take the shine off it.
ADAM	Eiffel may have built a bigger tower but he didn't have a circus underneath.
NANCY	You hate circuses. The clowns terrify you.
ADAM	Isn't everyone afraid of clowns? Those fixed grins and greased up faces, classic nightmare material. It took us two fucking hours to find each other amongst all those tourists.
NANCY	But we did find each other, eventually. I heard you first. Trying to buy a baguette from a stall as I remember. You'd lost your temper.
ADAM	I was trying to make myself understood. Armed with only my pigeon French and bilingual finger. If you don't know the word, simply point. I was desperate for a cheese sandwich. My blood sugar level was way out.
NANCY	Nothing to do with the amount of wine you had consumed the night before.
ADAM	Possibly, but who would be a vegetarian in France? It's so difficult to find something to eat which doesn't shit or have a mother. The French

	simply don't understand what a vegetarian is.
NANCY	Actually, they do. They just don't know <u>why</u> a vegetarian is. That's not what sticks in my mind about that weekend.
ADAM	Our anniversary, I remember.
NANCY	How we celebrated.
ADAM	How we argued.
NANCY	I love a fighter. It's a cliché but the bad boy image always attracts... *(holding his bruised face)*...especially when it has such a vulnerable centre.
ADAM	Any regrets?
NANCY	We were good together. *(smiles in thought)* Sometimes.
ADAM	I do miss you.
NANCY	Snap.
ADAM	After all that has happened… I don't want to be on my own. Not tonight.
NANCY	You don't have to be.

They embrace and, after a few moments hugging, start to kiss.
Their kissing becomes more passionate and their caresses
more intimate.

ADAM   Let's go upstairs.

ADAM's words seem to break the spell of intimacy between
them and NANCY pulls away realising she is making a
mistake.

NANCY   That's not a good idea.

ADAM   *(Looking hurt and puzzled)* Why?

NANCY   *(NANCY straightens her clothing)*
                        Cressida is asleep.

ADAM   I can say goodnight to her on the way
                        up. I haven't seen her for …

NANCY   …You can see her in the morning. I
                        don't want her disturbed.

ADAM   You don't trust me?

NANCY   To do what exactly? Look I don't want
                        to wake her. End of story.

ADAM   When I told the police how much I
                        loved Cress, do you want to know what
                        they asked me? How I showed that
                        love. Did I cuddle her, kiss her, touch
                        her? What kind of world are we living
                        in when a father can no longer have
                        any physical contact with his kids

without the suspicion of something sexual being involved?

NANCY   I do understand but you have to see things from my side as well. If you must know, I'm taking a huge risk by bringing Cressida here.

ADAM   What?

NANCY   Social Services contacted me regarding your access to her. You're on the Sex Offenders Register, for Gods sake and will be for the next two years.

ADAM   I don't believe this is happening. I'm not guilty, haven't been put before a jury, but I'm lumped in, along with convicted rapists, flashers and perverts. Is that why you won't let me near my own daughter?

NANCY stands up and faces ADAM.

NANCY   It's out of control Adam, it's taken on a life of its own.

ADAM   But I'm innocent. I was pressurised into accepting the police caution.

NANCY   You wouldn't listen to the legal advice...you never do listen.

ADAM   It was the only way I felt I could get out of the situation. I was frightened,

	felt cornered...I wasn't thinking straight.
NANCY	But that's just it. You took the decision to accept the caution, despite advice. And now Social Services are involved and our case, our family, is flagged. It no longer matters what it is right, wrong or even fair.......
	.....We have to be so careful, Adam.
ADAM	Not to leave me on my own in case I abuse her?
NANCY	That's not what I mean and you know it.
ADAM	It's what they mean though. First Charlotte and now you. Why don't you leave, with Cress, I'm obviously dangerous to be around.
NANCY	Don't be unreasonable, Adam.
ADAM	Lock me away, castrate me, then throw away the key. I've been written off as a member of the human race.

ADAM lies back down on the sofa facing away from NANCY.

NANCY	I can't talk to you when you're in this kind of mood. I'm going back to bed.
ADAM	*(Angrily)* Turn out the fucking light.

SCENE 3

Photographic images of an English school yard are projected onto the stage wall.

The yard is empty of children but we do hear the sounds of children playing.

SCENE 4

Nancy's flat. Late afternoon. STEPHEN GILES is sat at a table in the Kitchen. He is working at a laptop. The back door is flung open. ADAM, looking flustered, storms in. He sees STEPHEN.

ADAM   Where is she?

STEPHEN   With her mother.

ADAM sits at the table across from STEPHEN. He says nothing. STEPHEN attempts to ignore him and carries on typing. After a few moments painful silence ADAM reaches over and closes the lid of STEPHEN'S laptop.

ADAM   What are you doing here?

STEPHEN lifts ADAM's hand away from the laptop and re-opens it.

STEPHEN   I'm working. Or at least I was until you
                        interrupted me. What are you doing
                        here?

                        (ADAM ignores STEPHEN)

                        Why are you here?

ADAM   Don't you think such existential...

STEPHEN   *(Interrupting ADAM and cutting him off
                        in mid-sentence)* ...Spare me your
                        pseudo intellectual jibes. They may fool
                        your students but they bore me. And

	they don't hide the fact that you are evading the question.
ADAM	What business is it of yours anyway?
STEPHEN	You have just burst into my home.
ADAM	Your home?
STEPHEN	Indeed.
ADAM	And what contribution have you made to it?
STEPHEN	It's an ongoing project on my part.
ADAM	I've put more into…

STEPHEN interrupts ADAM.

STEPHEN	…and Nancy bought out your share - such as it was. And whilst we are on the subject of just whose home it is; Nancy wants the keys back.
ADAM	What does Nancy see in you?
STEPHEN	A father for Cress, perhaps.
ADAM	Fuck you!
STEPHEN	Still as eloquent as ever. The keys… please.
ADAM	I need a drink.

(ADAM gets up from the table and goes to a cupboard. He opens it and, without closing it, opens another, then another. He cannot find what he is looking for)

…we used to keep the…

STEPHEN   Things have changed since this ceased to be your home. People move on. So should you.

ADAM   Thanks for the advice.

STEPHEN   Let her go.

ADAM   To make things easier for you? Fuck that.

STEPHEN   You cannot seriously be saying that you are putting her in this position to somehow spite me.

ADAM   Is that what you think?

STEPHEN   Of late it has been difficult to comprehend your motives. Stop for a moment and think what you are doing to her.

ADAM   I'm not out to hurt Nancy and there is no...

STEPHEN interrupts ADAM angrily - slapping his hand on the table.

STEPHEN   …You are hurting her.

                     (ADAM looks shocked but he cannot
                     find the words to respond)

                     And you are not doing yourself any
                     favours either.

ADAM   As if you are interested in my welfare.

STEPHEN   Admittedly only so far as it impacts
                     upon mine.

ADAM   I'll impact upon you if you don't butt
                     out.

STEPHEN gestures towards ADAM's facial wounds.

STEPHEN   And that method of solving your
                     problems has always proved so
                     successful. Move on with at least some
                     dignity left…

                     (STEPHEN breaks off the sentence as
                     he sees that he may be pushing ADAM a
                     bit too far and doesn't want a fight to
                     break out in the family home. ADAM is
                     also standing which puts STEPHEN at a
                     disadvantage because he is still sat at
                     the table should a fight break out)

                     Adam. You're a photographer and
                     therefore supposed to be observant.
                     Open your eyes. See how your stupid

stubborn streak is affecting others. Cress, for example.

ADAM

Don't you dare mention my daughters name or even think to advise me as to her welfare.

STEPHEN

Fair enough. It falls on deaf ears anyway. You've ignored the advice from your solicitor, from Nancy and…

ADAM

You always have had an eye for Nancy. You just couldn't handle it that she married me and not you.

STEPHEN

All good things come to those that wait.

ADAM

I still love her.

STEPHEN

So much so that she ended up divorcing you for cheating on her. It isn't love you feel for her. It's dependency. You fear that without Nancy you will be nothing.

ADAM

(Dismissively) If you say so.

STEPHEN

That is why you will not hand over the negatives.

ADAM

What?

STEPHEN

You are using them as way to try hang on to, and control, Nancy. It isn't about freedom of speech at all.

ADAM   *(Laughs)* You really don't feel secure in
                        your relationship with Nancy.

STEPHEN   Would it help you deal with your
                        jealousy if I were to pretend that was the
                        case?

ADAM   You're threatened because she still has
                        feelings for me.

STEPHEN   She pities you. Why on earth would I
                        feel threatened by someone she feels
                        pity towards?

ADAM   She doesn't...

STEPHEN interrupts ADAM.

STEPHEN   ...I can tell from your face that you
                        know I am right. You should also know
                        that you make her feel ashamed.

                        *(ADAM looks devastated and struggles
                        to say anything. Despite being in a
                        vulnerable position whilst sat at the
                        table, STEPHEN cannot resist sticking
                        the knife in deeper)*

                        ...She is ashamed of you.

                        *(Still no response from a shocked and
                        hurt ADAM)*

                        ...Isn't this where you respond with
                        something witty like 'Fuck you'

…Lost for words?

(ADAM looks close to tears)

…OK. I've made my point.

…The keys were a courtesy that has since been withdrawn.

STEPHEN holds out his hand expectantly.

ADAM   *(Angrily)* You want them? OK. If it makes you feel any safer. Here – have them.

ADAM throws the keys onto the floor.

STEPHEN   You brought it all upon yourself. For as long as I have known you; you've always ended up biting the hand that feeds you. You're in danger of losing everything and everyone.

(ADAM gives a look that STEPHEN interprets as "I need no one.")

You can try to convince yourself that you need no one but there is nothing heroic in being alone. Anyway - what about Charlotte?

ADAM   She means nothing.

ADAM exits NANCY'S flat.

STEPHEN gets up from the table and calmly picks up the keys and, smiling to himself, places them on an empty hook of the key rack. He then opens a cupboard that ADAM had failed to look into in his search for a drink. From this cupboard STEPHEN takes out a bottle of scotch and a glass. He pours himself a drink and his smile intensifies.

SCENE 5

ADAM's studio.

ADAM stands in only his underwear and socks. He is looking dishevelled, unshaven and has obviously let himself go. His face still shows signs of the fight earlier. He has been drinking.

Empty wine bottles can be seen on stage. There are also a couple of medicine/pill containers – anti-depressants.

ADAM projects various slides onto the studio wall. The first slide is of a young naked child running towards a tree in a park - it is the same photograph that D.S. TURNER commented upon in the police interview. ADAM puts on a dressing gown and sits in a chair.

He picks up a recently purchased TABLET PC and taps at the on-screen keyboard.

CHARLOTTE enters.

CHARLOTTE	Adam…
	(No response from ADAM)
	…I didn't go. To Paris, I mean.
ADAM	Clearly.
CHARLOTTE	I couldn't board the plane to leave. I couldn't leave you.

ADAM   I don't need your pity, I've plenty of
                        my own.

*CHARLOTTE approaches ADAM. It is the first time she has
seen the bruising on his face from the fight.*

CHARLOTTE   What's happened to your face?

ADAM   *(ADAM rebuffs CHARLOTTES
                        approach)* Sorry. You could start by
                        saying sorry.

CHARLOTTE   I've been staying with friends.

ADAM   So you said in your text messages.

CHARLOTTE   You got them. You didn't reply to any
                        of them. I was worried about you. I …

ADAM   You thought that you had a right to a
                        reply?

CHARLOTTE   I deserve that much, surely.

ADAM   Do you? OK…

                        *(ADAM reaches for a mobile phone.
                        He selects messages and reads them
                        out)*

                        "I couldn't board the plane. I'm getting
                        a Taxi back. Call me when you pick
                        this up."

                        My response is …'delete'

(ADAM deletes the message from the phone)

"This is hurting me so much. Why don't you answer?"

My answer is …'delete'

(ADAM deletes the message from the phone)

"I need to know that you are OK. I love you"

You had a fine way of showing it…'delete'

(ADAM deletes the message from the phone)

Do I need to go on?

CHARLOTTE   No.

ADAM   Why stop there…remember these?

"Morning babe. I long to be in…"

CHARLOTTE snatches the phone away from ADAM before he can finish.

CHARLOTTE   Stop it. How can you be so cruel?

ADAM   I'm told it's one of my many talents.

CHARLOTTE stands with her back to ADAM. She is shaking and clearly upset. An awkward silence follows that is finally broken when the land line telephone begins to ring. ADAM does not respond to it.

CHARLOTTE   Don't you want to know who it is?

ADAM   No.

CHARLOTTE makes towards the phone.

ADAM   *(shouting)* Leave it.

CHARLOTTE   What if it's important?

ADAM   I decide what is and what isn't important in this house. You gave up that right when you packed your suitcase.

CHARLOTTE   I made a mistake, I was wrong. I'm sorry.

ADAM   Thank you. Now you can leave. Goodbye.

CHARLOTTE   I needed time to think.

ADAM   That's what's so fucking hard to take. You actually had to think about it. You believed, even for a short while, I was capable of doing this.

CHARLOTTE   Nancy told me about Greening and the *(pause)* solicitors' letters.

ADAM	It's not about Nancy, it's not about Tony Greening or the fucking solicitors' letters; it's about a fundamental trust between the two of us.
CHARLOTTE	Please Adam, stop shouting.

ADAM's seems to mellow. CHARLOTTE is someone he can unburden himself on.

ADAM	My career has now crashed and burned.
CHARLOTTE	That's enough, Adam.
ADAM	The diary is full of cancellations, the publishers are calling off the book launch and most of my equipment's been seized. So which ever way you slice it, I'm ruined.
CHARLOTTE	I'll help clear your name. Prove to you how much I love you. We can take this on together.
ADAM	Why?
CHARLOTTE	So you forgive me and in return I will forgive you.
ADAM	For what?
CHARLOTTE	Last night. I came round to see you. I saw Nancy's car parked here so I stood outside in the rain for hours wondering

what to do. I watched you and Nancy through the window. You made love on the sofa.

ADAM   We did not.

CHARLOTTE   Don't deny it, I saw you with my own eyes.

ADAM   Like everybody else, you saw what you wanted to see. .

CHARLOTTE   I understand why. You were hurting and I was not there for you.

ADAM   Everyone seems to read me so well lately.

CHARLOTTE   When you needed comfort and support, you obviously turned to someone who could give you that. It should have been me.

ADAM   I didn't make love to Nancy...I...she doesn't trust me to be with...

ADAM starts to break down in tears.

CHARLOTTE   It doesn't matter. *(CHARLOTTE goes over to ADAM)* I'm here for you now.

CHARLOTTE and ADAM embrace.

ADAM   What am I going to do Charlotte? I'm fucked.

CHARLOTTE	We go to the press. Put across your side of the story. We explain about the Tony Greening connection, of how you were threatened if you did not remove the photographs of his daughter…
ADAM	We can't prove it, Charlotte. He's been far too clever and he has people protecting him.
CHARLOTTE	…you've had personal property confiscated. You've been forced to accept a caution and they've demanded you hand over negatives. Sounds like a great news story to me. Especially with an election due.
ADAM	I want this to end. No more headlines.
CHARLOTTE	That doesn't sound like the Adam I know.
ADAM	I'm the perfect target. I teach. Sometimes photograph children and some of my other images are erotic. And lets face it I do have a bit of a gob…

(The telephone rings again, ADAM picks up the receiver and immediately slams it back down)

If I read a newspaper article about myself, I'd suspect I was guilty for fuck's sake. I'm not even sure if…

(becoming more upset and agitated)… You didn't see what the police showed me.

CHARLOTTE

You have to defend yourself.

(CHARLOTTE picks up a wine bottle and holds it up to ADAM)

And you will not find the answer in here.

ADAM

It helps…

CHARLOTTE

…only to make matters worse… nothing more.

(CHARLOTTE puts down the bottle and picks up a pill bottle)

And you should not be drinking whilst taking these.

ADAM

I thought it was a game. They changed the stakes and I've lost it all. I thought I'd lost you.

CHARLOTTE

We will work this out together..

ADAM

No. I can't risk it all blowing up in my face again.

CHARLOTTE

We have to at least try.

ADAM

I also have to think of Cress. I don't want her hurt by any more stories about how horrible her dad is.

CHARLOTTE

I understand that...we can discuss it all later but right now... you look a mess, Adam.

ADAM

Thanks.

CHARLOTTE

I bet you've not eaten.

ADAM

I had something ...

CHARLOTTE

You have had nothing but booze. How about I make dinner whilst you go and clean yourself up? We can talk more later; when you are feeling better. How does that sound?

There is a knock at the door. After a few moments CHARLOTTE goes over to see who it is. It is D.C.I. LYDON and D.S. TURNER. Ignoring CHARLOTTE, they enter.

D.S.TURNER

Mr Lazenby.

ADAM

Christ! It's our favourite friends from the local Gestapo. We are going to have to stop meeting like this. If we are not careful people are going to start to talk…

D.S.TURNER

Where were you at three fifty yesterday afternoon?

ADAM	Can't remember.
D.C.I. LYDON	If I can ask you not to be flippant, Sir. Please, answer the question.
ADAM	I do apologise but I've been under a great deal of mental strain recently. You may have read about me in the papers. "Society Photographer Linked to Paedophile Ring", "Sick Snapper's Sex Studio", etc. etc.
D.C.I. LYDON	We have reason to believe you were in the vicinity of St Mary's School for Girls.
ADAM	Was I?
D.C.I. LYDON	You were seen by a number of parents and the headmistress.
ADAM	Perhaps it was someone who looks like me.
D.C.I. LYDON	St Mary's is your daughter's school, is it not?
ADAM	Yes!
CHARLOTTE	Adam, what is…
ADAM	(ADAM addresses CHARLOTTE) I was trying to pick Cress up…surprise her and take her to the cinema.

D.C.I. LYDON	All things considered, was that really wise?
ADAM	She is _my_ daughter.
D.C.I. LYDON	Social Services have ordered that you have restricted access to your daughter.
ADAM	*(Addressing CHARLOTTE)* It was a waste of time anyway - Cress had been kept away from school. She's upset that her father has been labelled a child pornographer and she's being bullied by some of the older girls. Are *(ADAM turns and points at D.C.I. LYDON)* you satisfied that in your job of protecting children, you have done untold damage to the one child I care most about?
D.C.I. LYDON	I'm sorry if your daughter has been upset.
ADAM	*(Dismissively)* But of course you are…

CHARLOTTE approaches ADAM and stands by him, taking his hand in hers.

CHARLOTTE	*(Addressing D.C.I. LYDON)* Can't it wait – this isn't the best time. Could you not come back tomorrow?
D.C.I. LYDON	I'm afraid not. We have received a complaint from one of the parents that Mr Lazenby verbally and physically assaulted him.

ADAM   Bollocks.

D.C.I. LYDON   He received a blow to his chest and is
                        quite insistent on pressing charges.

ADAM   *(Directed towards CHARLOTTE)* I was
                        waiting for my daughter and this twat
                        gave me some verbal and I reacted like
                        any other man. I told him to go and
                        fuck himself. *(Directed towards D.C.I.
                        LYDON)* As for hitting him, I merely
                        pushed him out of the way so I could
                        enter the school yard.

CHARLOTTE   Oh, Adam!

CHARLOTTE slumps onto the sofa, upset.

ADAM   He was blocking my path.

D.S. TURNER   Mr Lazenby, can we talk privately?

CHARLOTTE gets up to leave the room.

ADAM   She's staying here.

CHARLOTTE returns and stands by ADAM's side.

D.S. TURNER   Mr Lazenby, you cannot go around
                        assaulting people…

ADAM   Why should I have to put up with the
                        things he said?

D.C.I. LYDON	I know it must be hard to deal with the gossip and the reactions from people but you must see that this could all be cleared up to everyone's satisfaction by simply handing over the negatives.
ADAM	Never.
D.C.I. LYDON	Why put yourself under any more strain than is necessary?
ADAM	As if you care.
D.C.I.LYDON	You really do go out of your way to make things more difficult for yourself. We know that you have corresponded further with Collins.
	(D.C.I. LYDON picks up the TABLET PC and hands it to D.S. TURNER)
	We have been monitoring his accounts and noted messages from you.
CHARLOTTE	Who is Collins?
ADAM	I was warning him to be careful.
D.C.I.LYDON	You were warning him? About this investigation?
ADAM	No, to be careful of me. Of what I intend to do. None of my images are going to be linked with his kind of filth.

D.C.I. LYDON signals to D.S. TURNER who moves towards ADAM.

D.C.I. LYDON   I think we should continue this at the station.

ADAM   I'm going nowhere.

D.S. TURNER is now behind ADAM.

CHARLOTTE   *(Protesting)* Can't you see he is both tired and ill? Let him sleep and we will come to the station first thing in the morning. I will make sure he attends.

D.C.I.LYDON   I can see that he has been drinking. Is he on any medication or has he taken anything else?

CHARLOTTE   Other than what his Doctor prescribed, no. Not that I am aware of.

D.C.I.LYDON   He'll be seen by the duty Doctor, as is his right, but I must insist that he comes with us.

D.S. TURNER takes hold of ADAM by his arm and gently starts to lead ADAM away.

D.S.TURNER   Come along Sir. *(There is a very brief struggle but ADAM clearly has little fight left in him. D.S. TURNER takes a softer approach)*…Please.

CHARLOTTE intervenes.

CHARLOTTE   Adam. Best go with them. I'll call
                 Nancy. She'll know what to do.

*ADAM is led away by D.S. TURNER out of the studio,
followed by D.C.I. LYDON, leaving CHARLOTTE alone. The
telephone begins to ring. CHARLOTTE stands there not quite
knowing what to do. The phone continues to ring as the lights
fade.*

SCENE 6

Inside NANCY and STEPHENS flat – Kitchen.

NANCY and STEPHEN GILES enter. We join them mid-conversation.

NANCY   No!

STEPHEN   Why? You need to start being more selfish, Nancy. Think about yourself for a change.

NANCY   You think I'm putting my life on hold for him?

STEPHEN   *(Angrily)* No! You are putting <u>our</u> lives on hold. *(Regaining his composure)* I'm sorry… *(STEPHEN sits at the table)*…he's not exactly been slow to move on. Did he think of your feelings each time he paraded his latest model in front of you? No.

NANCY   That's just the way he is.

NANCY takes an opened bottle of wine and two glasses.

STEPHEN   Stop making excuses for him. You don't owe him anything and I certainly don't.

NANCY places a glass in front of STEPHEN and pours wine into it. NANCY sits at the table across from STEPHEN - she pours herself a glass of wine as she speaks.

NANCY	I may no longer be his wife, Stephen, but I am still his friend.
STEPHEN	Well he isn't mine.
NANCY	You were good friends once.
STEPHEN	A long time ago. And he's used up any get out of jail privileges a former friendship may grant. *(Angrily and with raised voice)* He needs to stop behaving like Peter fucking Pan.
NANCY	*(Soft but harsh)* Keep your voice down. You will wake Cressida. *(Then in a firmer tone)* I'll tell him when I feel the time is right to do so and not before.
STEPHEN	Meanwhile Adam takes centre stage once again. Just where he loves to be.
NANCY	Now who needs to grow up?
STEPHEN	You do want this relationship to work, don't you Nancy?
NANCY	Of course I do but for the time being we've just go to …
STEPHEN	…carry on regardless?
	(Pause – waiting for a response from NANCY that doesn't come)

How do you think that makes me feel? You haven't even discussed it with Cress.

NANCY

I realise that it is difficult but you have to understand.

STEPHEN

I'm trying but I don't know how much longer I can wait for Adam to get his act together.

NANCY

I was talking about Cressida.

STEPHEN

Right. Of course.

NANCY

We will have to take things slowly with her. After all, when we are married you'll end up seeing more of her than Adam will.

STEPHEN

And I have no intention of taking his place, but that doesn't mean that there should be any problems with Cress being a part of our lives together.

NANCY

Adam won't see it that way. Not in his present state of mind.

STEPHEN

(Sharply) He will have to. *(STEPHEN pauses and then proceeds in a calmer tone)* OK, I can understand you not telling Adam at present but it isn't just him you are keeping it from. You will not allow anyone to know that we are engaged. How do you think I feel when

I see you take off the ring when you go out?

NANCY   Don't read anything into that. I simply don't like wearing jewellery at work

STEPHEN   But you have no problem wearing his necklace.

NANCY   Stephen, we agreed to…

STEPHEN   …take things slowly I know. But we don't seem to be making any move forward and that is because Adam is getting away with setting the agenda.

NANCY   He's seeing threats everywhere.

STEPHEN   And whose fault's that?

NANCY   He's been something of a recluse since the night of the fight.

STEPHEN   The experience didn't knock any sense into him, I bet.

NANCY   I don't understand how people can do this. It's frightening.

STEPHEN   He accepted the police caution, against the advice of his solicitor, and many will see that as an admission of guilt.

NANCY   And that is an excuse for people to act like vigilantes?

STEPHEN	I'm not saying it is, Nancy. We may think it's unfair but there are those who will see him as guilty. You have to accept that. And, if he had any sense, so would he.
NANCY	What do you believe?
STEPHEN	I've said, I believe it is time for...?
NANCY	*(NANCY cuts off STEPHEN)* I mean what do you believe? About Adam, do you think he is guilty? It's just that... you have never really said.
STEPHEN	Look. I've made my feelings about Adam very plain. I think he is immature, self-centred, arrogant...but a paedophile, well, I find that hard to believe. I do have one concern though.
NANCY	And that is?
STEPHEN	I do know about what happened to Adam as a child. As you have said, we were once friends. I've been thinking...is it possible Adam had been looking at ways of exploring or investigating what he experienced as a kid...and in the process he became caught up in something? *(Seeing NANCY's pained expression)* I'm just trying to...look...If only Adam would just hand over those bloody negatives maybe we could all carry on with our

lives? End of story... Have you seen all of them?

NANCY   I've seen the proofs and a few contacts, that's all.

STEPHEN   Nancy...?

NANCY   That is how he normally works, nothing strange in that.

STEPHEN   Stand aside from it all for a moment. Be objective. Could he have overstepped the mark and that is why he's scared of handing them over?

NANCY   Never.

STEPHEN   Are you 100% sure?

NANCY   Absolutely. Besides he has promised he'll retrieve them from storage, so that I can hand them over to the police.

STEPHEN   At last! Typical of him to get you to do his dirty work though.

NANCY   I am his agent.

STEPHEN   So, as his agent, make sure you hold him to his promise.

NANCY   How I deal with my clients is my business, Stephen.

STEPHEN	You do have other clients that you represent. Have you thought about how this is affecting them?
NANCY	Of course I have.
STEPHEN	They must have spoken to you about it.
NANCY	That is none of your business.
STEPHEN	OK. But have you stopped to think how you look to others? After all, it is your agency name that is mentioned in the press reports.
NANCY	Don't you think I know that?
STEPHEN	I never hear you talk about how all this is impacts upon you. You are far too busy defending Adam. It isn't just how it looks for you professionally. What about Social Services?
NANCY	What about them?
STEPHEN	You have to consider how they view your unquestioning support of Adam.
NANCY	My unquestioning support?
STEPHEN	That is how it might look to some.
NANCY	And to you?
STEPHEN	That isn't what I meant.

NANCY   Isn't it? You obviously don't know me
                 as well as you thought.

*Off stage we hear a child moving up stairs and calling down
for NANCY.*

CRESSIDA   Mum.

NANCY   *(To STEPHEN)* Shit!

                 (calling off stage) OK, hon, I'm
                 coming.

                 (to STEPHEN) Are you happy now?

                 (NANCY exits stage)

STEPHEN   Fucking delirious.

SCENE 7

ADAM's studio. ADAM is sat down on the sofa. His actions and responses show that he is still clearly not with it and is withdrawn. His depression has become deeper and is under increased medication from his doctors.

CHARLOTTE enters carrying a box. She moves over to Adam and sits down beside him.

CHARLOTTE   Hi you...

                   (ADAM doesn't respond.
                   CHARLOTTE tenderly runs her hands
                   through ADAM's hair).

                   I know you are in there somewhere.

                   (CHARLOTTE playfully taps him on
                   his head)

                   Wake up lover...I have something for
                   you.

CHARLOTTE passes the box to ADAM. She has to place it in his hands due to his slow response.

ADAM   What is it?

CHARLOTTE   Open it and see...

                   (ADAM first just looks at the package.
                   CHARLOTTE has to encourage him to

open the box. He slowly opens it and takes out a camera)

…I know it's nowhere near as good as your others but it is something you can use until you get them back from the po…

(CHARLOTTE was to say 'police' but thinks better of it and lets that trail off)

…I saw this in the shop window and thought it might help. It's second-hand, I know, but I couldn't afford much. It's a film camera, none of that digital muck. The guy in the shop said it was considered a classic model. What do you think?

ADAM   I used to have one like this.

CHARLOTTE   So it is a good camera?

ADAM   Yes.

CHARLOTTE   Great. See, I do listen to you when you go on about this and that camera…

(CHARLOTTE jumps to her feet)

Let's test it out.

ADAM   What?

CHARLOTTE   Do a shoot now.

ADAM   I'm not in the mood.

CHARLOTTE   Oh, come on...for me, please.

ADAM   Maybe, later.

CHARLOTTE   Why not now? I'm all excited. I want
                to see if I made a good purchase.

ADAM   Photograph what?

CHARLOTTE   Me, of course, silly!

ADAM   The film's still in the freezer. No time
                to defrost it.

CHARLOTTE   I've thought of that as well...

                *(CHARLOTTE produces a couple of
                rolls of film from her pocket and
                holds them up to ADAM)*

                ...I took some out last night.

ADAM   You think of everything, don't you?

CHARLOTTE   Yep! Annoying isn't it?

                *(CHARLOTTE takes ADAM's hand
                and pulls him up off the couch)*

                Come on then.

ADAM   *(Shaking his head)* I'm too tired,
                Charlotte. Tomorrow?

CHARLOTTE	For the past few weeks you've not made a single image.
ADAM	And that surprises you?
CHARLOTTE	You have to start again at some point. So why not now? Let's go out for a walk. The light's great today.

(ADAM just gently shakes his head – staring down at the camera – rolling it in his hands – pretending to show interest in it in an attempt to ignore CHARLOTTE)

	Bright but overcast…wrap around lighting. Very flattering. We can take the camera to the park and you can photograph me by the pond.
ADAM	*(quietly)* No.
CHARLOTTE	A couple of hours fun.

CHARLOTTE walks across stage to get ADAM's jacket and hands it to him.

ADAM	*(sharply)* No!
CHARLOTTE	Why not? It will do you good to get out of the house. Just for the afternoon. It'll help clear your head.
ADAM	I'm not being seen…not with a camera. I don't feel right.

135

CHARLOTTE   You'll feel better with some fresh air.

ADAM   People might get the wrong idea.

CHARLOTTE   You are worried what people might
              think?...I know it's difficult but by
              letting simple-minded fools stop you
              from getting on with your life – they
              win.

ADAM   It's not safe for me to be...

CHARLOTTE   Adam...

              *(CHARLOTTE realises she will not get
              ADAM out of the house)*

              ...Okay, I understand...

              *(CHARLOTTE looks around the studio
              flat.)*

              We can work here! We don't have to
              do anything elaborate.

              (CHARLOTTE tries to sound upbeat)

              How about a few head and shoulder
              shots with the available light?

              *(CHARLOTTE moves across the studio
              and takes a studio stool)*

              Over here?

ADAM   I…

CHARLOTTE   Just a couple of rolls.

ADAM   Will it shut you up?

CHARLOTTE   *(smiling)* It might…

                (ADAM tries to load a camera with film but makes a mess of it. CHARLOTTE takes the camera off him)

                …Give it here.

                (CHARLOTTE loads the film in the camera and gives it back to ADAM who just stares at it. Charlotte sits on the stool.)

                (Playfully) How do you want me?

                (No response from ADAM)

                …What no suggestive comeback? Even when I set them up for you. What am I going to do with you?

ADAM hasn't put the camera to his eye. CHARLOTTE has to prompt him to do so. She walks over to him and playfully takes his arm and bends it until the camera is in position in front of his face.

CHARLOTTE   OK, I have learned enough from you to know that the camera goes here…

(CHARLOTTE stands up on her toes to playfully 'look' through the lens at the front of the camera that is now at ADAM's eye)

Correct position now assumed, sir!

(CHARLOTTE walks back to the stool)

Ready?

(CHARLOTTE spends time attempting to gain ADAM's interest by making several playful poses – sending up modelling and trying to lighten the mood. ADAM now has the camera to his eye but is not interested in shooting)

Not inspiring you…clearly I'm losing my touch.

(Losing her battle to snap ADAM out of his mood)

Why don't you suggest a pose?

(No response from ADAM)

Adam? Talk to me. Please.

ADAM   It doesn't feel right…the camera…

CHARLOTTE gets up from the stool and approaches ADAM.

CHARLOTTE   You don't like it? But you had one like
               this…I can exchange it if…

ADAM   It's not that.

CHARLOTTE   What is it then?

ADAM   It feels…it's alien. It doesn't belong. I
               don't …

*ADAM puts down the camera and walks away from it and out
of the studio leaving CHARLOTTE alone on stage. Looking
defeated, CHARLOTTE picks up her bag and exits the stage.
Lights fade.*

SCENE 8

Inside ADAM's studio. It is stripped bare and the few remaining items lie strewn around the floor. ADAM, sat on the sofa, stares into space.

NANCY　　　　　　　　*(off stage)* Adam? You there?

ADAM doesn't answer. NANCY enters.

NANCY　　　　　　　　Adam…How are you doing?

ADAM　　　　　　　　All things considered, I'm coping.

NANCY　　　　　　　　*(Looking around the studio - NANCY picks up a few items off the floor and attempts to tidy up)*

　　　　　　　　　　　It looks like it. Any plans for today?

ADAM　　　　　　　　I'm waiting.

NANCY　　　　　　　　For what?

ADAM　　　　　　　　The next bombshell.

STEPHEN enters.

ADAM　　　　　　　　*(Looking at STEPHEN)* What the fuck is he doing here?

STEPHEN　　　　　　　*(Addressing NANCY)* I told you this wasn't a good idea. Best I wait in the car.

NANCY   *(Addressing STEPHEN)* Stay.

                 (STEPHEN takes a seat across from ADAM)

                 (to ADAM) Stephen has suggested we go to his paper…

ADAM   …Stephen has 'suggested'.

NANCY   Please, listen to what he has to say.

ADAM   *(dismissively)* I'm listening.

STEPHEN   My editor is sympathetic and is interested in an exclusive interview.

NANCY   See it as a chance for you to put forward your side of the story.

                 (ADAM doesn't respond)

                 It could work in our favour if we play it right.

ADAM   *(Pointing to both STEPHEN and NANCY)* When you say 'work in our favour' you mean it will serve to benefit you two. No!

STEPHEN   We are wasting our time. He isn't prepared to…

NANCY   *(NANCY puts up a hand to STEPHEN signalling him to be quiet)*

	Think before you refuse, Adam.
ADAM	I gave it all the thought Stephens 'suggestion' deserved – there was no need for more.
NANCY	How is all this affecting Cressida? On top of all she's had to face already.
ADAM	*(Stands up from the sofa)* Why bring Cress into this?
NANCY	It could draw a line under all this and ease things for her at school. The sooner it is all ended the better.
ADAM	You're using her to force me to agree.
NANCY	I am advising you to say yes, as your agent.
ADAM	Advice noted.
NANCY	And your answer?
ADAM	The answer is no.
NANCY	Then there's no easy way of…I cannot represent you any longer.
ADAM	This is a joke, you are joking, aren't you?
NANCY	I'm afraid not.

ADAM	Fuck you.
	(Paces the room and then points to STEPHEN)
	Is this another one of <u>his</u> suggestions?
	(pacing about the room)
	How am I supposed to react, Nancy?
STEPHEN	You are not the only client she represents.
ADAM	You have done enough damage – I suggest that you keep quiet.
NANCY	The recent events have been affecting them as well.
ADAM	Oh really, tell me just how has it affected them exactly?
NANCY	They have been worried at the possibility of been associated with your problem.
ADAM	My problem? It's not our problem now?
NANCY	It has affected business.
ADAM	I'd have thought the notoriety would have had the opposite effect.

NANCY   Nobody wants to get...

ADAM/NANCY   *(together)* ...tarred with the same brush.

There is an awkward, uncomfortable silence.

STEPHEN   She does have a loyalty towards them
                         too. You have to take that…

*ADAM gives STEPHEN a look that causes STEPHEN to stop
mid sentence. After a pause ADAM turns to NANCY.*

ADAM   What about your loyalty to me?

NANCY   Adam, I would have done anything to
                         avoid this.

ADAM   *(Shouting angrily - causing NANCY to
                         back away from ADAM)* Well, fucking
                         try harder…

                         *(more restrained and with a hint of
                         pleading in ADAM's voice)* …I'm
                         your oldest client Nancy. You made
                         your name representing me.

STEPHEN   Be reasonable.

ADAM   *(Ignoring STEPHEN)* After all this
                         time, Christ, we've had our differences
                         but to do this to me? What kind of
                         message do you think this gives out to
                         the world?

NANCY	I'll put out a press release, stating that it is an amicable parting.
ADAM	Oh, spare me your fucking press release. There is nothing amicable about it. Why not put the truth out that even my ex-wife, the mother of my child, doesn't trust me?
NANCY	That's not true.
ADAM	This isn't just about sales and protecting your clients, is it? It's obvious that you're putting distance between us. Charlotte was right about you all along, how could I have been so naïve?
NANCY	Was it Charlotte who persuaded you to carry on with the book signing against my advice and that of your publishers? Look what a public relations disaster that became.
ADAM	How can you do this?
STEPHEN	Adam. Why don't you take some time out.
ADAM	What?
STEPHEN	Haven't you had an offer of a lecture spot in France? Why not take up that …

ADAM	*(moving aggressively towards STEPHEN)* …keep out of my fucking business. How many more times do…
STEPHEN	*(Rising from seat to meet ADAM)* …frightened that they have also seen through you and that you may have nowhere to left run…
NANCY	Stop it! The pair of you.
	(Addressing STEPHEN)
	Do you mind waiting in the car?
STEPHEN	Are you sure?
NANCY	There is something I need to discuss with Adam. Alone.
STEPHEN	I …
NANCY	Please. I will be out in a few minutes.

STEPHEN leaves the flat. There is an awkward silence.

NANCY	It's best you don't see Cressida for a while, until all this blows over.
ADAM	It just gets better and better. You cannot make a decision like that. She needs her father.
NANCY	She also needs protecting. As her father, you must see that.

ADAM	Cress gives me the strength to face all this. If I don't have her I've nothing to fight for.
NANCY	It'll only be for a short time.
ADAM	Nancy, I'm begging you, don't do this to me.
NANCY	I'll tell her you're going away on a shoot, for a few months. Go to Paris as you've been planning.
ADAM	I thought you no longer represented me?
NANCY	I'm trying to help.
ADAM	Keep out of planning my fucking life…

(long pause, ADAM is becoming more agitated. He paces room and then breaks silence)

…I'm Cress's father.

NANCY	And I am her mother.
ADAM	I know why you're doing this. I know about your engagement to *(ADAM points in direction of the door)* that fuckwit.
NANCY	I can't bear it when you're like this.

ADAM	Like what? Hurt, let down, betrayed? You're not stopping me from seeing Cress.
NANCY	I already have.
ADAM:	What?
	(pause)
NANCY	After your pathetic stunt outside her school, what did you expect me to do? Adam, she was interviewed by Social Services. She didn't speak for two days afterwards.
ADAM	*(Collapsing into the sofa)* Jesus.
NANCY	She sat in her room. Didn't eat, I couldn't go near her.
ADAM	*(Head in hands)* Oh please, what did they do to her?
NANCY	She only started talking about it this morning.
ADAM	What did those fucking bastards say?
NANCY	They wanted to know if you touched her.
ADAM	*(Looking up at NANCY in disbelief)* Touched her?

NANCY	They asked her if Daddy had touched her, touched her in a special way. Wanted to know if she knew the difference between 'good touching' and 'bad touching'.
ADAM	*(Standing up from the sofa)* You are kidding me?
NANCY	They also wanted to know if she had any secrets. Things that only she and her Daddy shared.
ADAM	What?
NANCY	You bastard. Look what you've done. *(NANCY starts to cry)* You stupid bastard, I told you we had to be careful.
ADAM	*(ADAM rushes to NANCY and holds her)* Nancy, I'm sorry. I would never have done anything like that, you must believe me.
NANCY	I do. I know. It's fucked up Adam, all of it.

They continue to hold each other. NANCY is crying.
CHARLOTTE enters.

CHARLOTTE	Adam? *(NANCY and ADAM part)*
NANCY	*(Backing away from ADAM)* Charlotte. Hello.

CHARLOTTE   I think you both should read this.
             (hands over a newspaper)

NANCY   What is it?

*ADAM reads for a second then throws the paper down.
NANCY picks it up and reads.*

CHARLOTTE   What do we do?

NANCY   At least we know where Greening
             stands.

ADAM   Hiding behind the safety of the party
             machine.

CHARLOTTE   Come to Paris. The press can be told
             this is a long standing engagement.

ADAM   It will look like I am running.

NANCY   No - It'll show you're still prepared to
             work.

CHARLOTTE   Nancy is right, it will also give you
             time to get your head together.

NANCY   And get your health back. I'll tell
             Cressida daddy's working. I'll take her
             to stay at her grandmother's. Get her
             out of London.

ADAM   And away from me.

NANCY	Stop twisting things. *(exasperated pause)* We can talk about this when you come back.
ADAM	Yes. Through my fucking solicitor. This isn't over. There will be no 'happy ever after' for you and Stephen. I'll see to that!
NANCY	If that's the way you want to play it. Fine. I tried.

NANCY leaves the stage. ADAM shouts after her.

ADAM	And give my regards to loverboy. Tell him, I will always be Cress's father. If he thinks he is going to take over… well he can think again.
	(ADAM moves quickly back to the sofa and sits down. He is agitated.)
	Tosser!

ADAM rocks gently whilst sat on the sofa. He is obviously annoyed and deep in thought.

After a long pause CHARLOTTE sits next to ADAM and, placing her hand on his shoulder, breaks the silence.

CHARLOTTE	Are you okay?
ADAM	Yes. I'm fine.
CHARLOTTE	You will sort things out with Nancy?

ADAM   (sharply) Yes…

                        (CHARLOTTE reacts to the tone of his
                        voice. ADAM, realising that he has
                        frightened her, places his hand on hers
                        and lowers his voice)

                        Forget Nancy.

ADAM gets up from the sofa and walks over to where files are
stored on a desk. He opens a file and takes out some negatives.
He leafs through them silently for a short period.

CHARLOTTE breaks the silence.

CHARLOTTE   Are those 'the' negatives?

ADAM   The ones of Emily Greening?

CHARLOTTE   Yes.

ADAM   Still that doubt, Charlotte? Do you
                        want to see, to make doubly sure,
                        that they are not pornographic?

CHARLOTTE   No.

ADAM   Take a look.

CHARLOTTE   What are you going to do with them?

ADAM   Haven't decided.

CHARLOTTE   But surely they can prove you're
                        innocence.

ADAM	Are you certain? Look. Answer those nagging doubts. I can see you're desperate to.

ADAM throws several negative glassine filing sheets, of 120 medium format, towards her.

CHARLOTTE	Please Adam, stop, you're scaring me.
ADAM	What are you scared of? Trust, Charlotte. Can you hand them back to me without looking? *(pause)* I'm waiting.

CHARLOTTE holds the negatives for a while, deciding, then hands them back without having examined them.

ADAM	Thank you.
CHARLOTTE	I don't understand why you…
ADAM	…haven't handed them over? *(ADAM shrugs)*
	No more questions. You have plans to make for us.
CHARLOTTE	I do?
ADAM	Paris.
CHARLOTTE	*(excitedly)* I should plan Paris?
ADAM	*(smiling)* Yeah, what the fuck. Let's do it. Just the two of us.

CHARLOTTE	You're sure?
ADAM	I am.
CHARLOTTE	For next month?
ADAM	Make the arrangements now. No sense in waiting. We can have that holiday first.
CHARLOTTE	It would be good to get away from here. I know a farmhouse we can book into.
ADAM	Let's get away this weekend. I will take the camera you bought me.
CHARLOTTE	Really?
ADAM	Can I leave you to organise it?
CHARLOTTE	I have some things to sort out and will call into that internet café on the way back to book the tickets. It will be quicker that way.

As CHARLOTTE is talking ADAM takes items out of his wallet and embraces CHARLOTTE from behind.

ADAM	Pay with that. *(ADAM hands CHARLOTTE a credit card. She takes it and smiles playfully)* Book business class and let's treat ourselves. Push the boat out, none of your budget airlines.

CHARLOTTE   You will be okay until I come back?

ADAM   *(smiling)* I have things to keep me
                occupied here.

CHARLOTTE goes over to ADAM and kisses him.

CHARLOTTE   I'll be as quick as I can.

ADAM   Don't worry about me. Take your time.
                I'm okay. Honest.

CHARLOTTE   You sure?

ADAM   Yes. Quick, before I change my mind.

*ADAM playfully chases her to the door slapping her bottom.
CHARLOTTE laughs as she is chased out of the room.*

*Upon re-entering the room ADAM's smile fades – it was
obviously for CHARLOTTE's benefit.*

*After a few moments thought he walks back to the desk and
takes some A4 35mm negatives sheets from a file and holds
each in turn up to the light. These are not the same negatives
he showed CHARLOTTE.*

*ADAM peruses them for a short while and then selects a pair
of negative sheets. He takes them and sits at a table, placing a
metal waste basket in position by his feet. Methodically he
takes a negative strip out of a sheet and, taking a cigarette
lighter, slowly burns the negatives. The lights fade leaving
only the light from the burning negatives to illuminate
ADAM's face. These burn out to leave the stage in darkness.*

THE END

THROWING STONES

Revised 2013 version.

What's in your family album?

Britannia Street Theatre and Arts Publishing

Look out for more arts and theatre titles from

Britannia Street Theatre and Arts Publishing

For more details email

britanniastreetartspublishing@gmail.com